NOVAHEAD

Steve Aylett is the author of
Slaughtermatic, LINT, Fain the Sorcerer,
Atom, The Crime Studio, Bigot Hall,
Rebel at the End of Time, Toxicology, The
Inflatable Volunteer, Shamanspace, And
Your Point Is?, The Complete Accomplice
and *Smithereens.*

NOVAHEAD

STEVE AYLETT

NOVAHEAD
by Steve Aylett

ISBN 978-0-9565677-2-7

Completed 2009, first published 2011

The final Beerlight novel

scargardenmedia@yahoo.co.uk

CONTENTS

"Fortune presents gifts
not according to the book."
- Luis De Góngora

"They couldn't hit an
elephant at this dist –"
- General John Sedgwick,
American Civil War

PART ONE

PANNA

1

BEERLIGHT STRANGER

I'd just flicked a spider off the desk, sighed and prepared to rise when the shadow of someone's head and shoulders appeared on the floor like the edge of a jigsaw piece. A galoot entered. His vibe was blank - I could see aura waste falling away from him like dead seeds. He even went with 'Prepare to die, Mister Atom.'

'Right this minute?' I asked, dubiously. 'It's not particularly convenient.'

His smile was incoherent, a dent in a sandbag. Maybe this was his favourite thing to do.

'Being bored by you better be worth it,' I told him. Probably my face bore the sort of amused and scornful look that people never like.

'You don't get to meet the Heber kid,' he said, then drew a sender like a riveted slab of tar. It was actually a Birch gun, the muzzle shored about with functionless flanges and baffles. He started firing the kind of bullets I preferred to see going the other way. Spent shells were flying like air quotes as I pulled the emergency cord and descended, the floor closing again above me. I'll open the ground when I choose.

I was surprised though. It had been ten years and I'd almost forgotten that stories still happened here, as if this world hadn't ended.

I'd known the town was finished when I put a phone to my ear and found it was a cockroach. I used to think rain sounded the same everywhere, falling on dead and undead. Before I got away and heard it on palms, reef ocean and blue air. And I should have stayed on the island. Now only a few hours back in town and I felt again it didn't matter where I was.

The one thing I hadn't considered was the risk of getting curious.

By the time I slanted the Mantarosa out of the parking lot the gun ape was ducking into a car consisting mainly of ribbed armour and roller bars. He headed portside and I followed with deadlights and a nightvision windshield. On the way out of Saints Street I sent the cleanup signal, at which my office jumped and settled into the ground, leaving only the sculpture of a construction site which a friend had fashioned on the roof. I'd miss the old place maybe.

Suddenly I was feeling cheerful. Neon was arcing down my spine and the scenery was springing out of my way. In a car like a straight razor, my rearview reflection backed by a pouring firewall that used to be my workplace. Trouble-bound under clenched heavens. Night windows like aquariums as I followed the cage car through the beginnings of rain toward the dead waterfront, centre of fish nostalgia and water canneries. I saw blue sparks kindling between my teeth.

He parked by the harbour wall and walked down a wooden ramp to a small shack which half-hung out over the sea. I stopped a way back and sat a while listening to the motor pinging as it settled. Cars with portholes are cool.

Rain was pouring into the sea and slashing off the vinyl roof of the hut. Under moonlight the walls were leaking silver. I walked over and took a look in the window. A fly-strip encrusted with bullets and a glass-fronted box on the wall with a sign saying FOR BROKEN GLASS BREAK GLASS. A little flaking wreck of a table. The only thing on it was one of those plastic plants that dance to gunfire, looking creepy in the weird light. But three fellas were propped around the table like carved dolls in a murky tank of turpentine. The gunsel was one. Sat on either side were a bucket-jawed giant with club bones and a little compacted guy with a round head and side-impact ears. And I thought, *What is it now?*

The button man was getting a dressing-down so elaborately phrased he probably thought he'd done good. The little guy was precise and petulant. 'We asked you to put him around a bullet, understand? To shoot him. And it wouldn't be unusual for him to die thereafter. If you haven't tried that experiment before you'll find there is something almost uncanny about the result.'

'That old detective front probably had a zero approach alarm, Mr Ract,' said the giant thoughtfully. 'He knew something was up the moment our verb-free associate entered the place.'

'What did you use, show me. What's that, a Birchy? Loud charm but slow on the uptake - it damn near fires by osmosis. If it had to be an ammo-guzzler why not a Barisal? Doesn't anyone use room-brooms anymore? Give it the once-over?'

The galoot looked sad. 'I can't have a big frenzy just like that Mr Ract.'

'My god, that's exactly the sort of frenzy you've *got* to have, man! I think this hitman of yours is some sort of manatee, Mr Darkwards. He's cert-ainly never been proven otherwise. And I haven't the patience for the gang talk.'

'It's how they get by,' said the giant calmly, nodding a head like a foundation stone. 'Mobster psychosis. It gives them a social structure, of sorts. Better than the wasteland outside, maybe.'

'Well we needn't really do it Beerlight style. Camouflage be damned, this is too important to leave to a - what do they call it here ... cleaner? Need I remind you if Atom and the boy meet it will be catastrophically interesting for me, you, and everyone in a five-hundred-mile radius.'

This gave me a bit of a start. I presented myself to this world as if by chance, the same as everyone else. Why such suspicion? I stood frowning in the smell of melted and rain-solidified rubber as the sad city went on losing its flavour like gum. Well, it didn't matter at this late stage. Something was leaping in me like old times.

Water murky as potion. A meeting of skulls behind a sizzling window. The gunsel hung back like a doughy robot, his eyes opaque and eager. I'd got a swatch on his aura. His mind was strange, thinking one thing at a time.

'He's getting near the city,' said the small man Ract, taking what looked like an elaborate jungle compass from a pocket and propping it on the table. 'According to the atomic clock. Where's our Mr Pivot? And has he selected an alternative conjecture or is he adamant?'

'The choreography of failure is infinitely varied,' drawled the giant.

'Does he understand the moral component of the exercise?'

'Is there one?'

'The hole where it should be is the right shape. It'll do.'

'Relax, Mr Ract. I'm told if you listen to one of his excuses while watching *The Wizard of Oz* it matches up in profound and hilarious ways. Anyway, since our willy-nilly friend here has failed by an order of magnitude we hadn't thought possible, we'll have to put Atom out of the game from another direction. Discrediting him with a bullet's all very well but -'

I ducked out and leopard-crawled unnecessarily back to the car, setting off through streets gummed with melted cellphones like cowchips.

Why was I rattling around Beerlight again? Its most precocious souls had escaped. Its colour had desaturated. It was mouthing old lines. Banal, undirected explosions were going off here and there. The city was crying out for the specific-rich carnage so beloved of the old-time accelerati. The days when crimes were written across the city like formulae, answering each other in a seemingly endless, dendritic conversation. But it would never see that inventiveness again, I thought.

I'll try to describe the beautiful ways I was wrong.

2

VALENTINE STREET

Buildings the colour of dried blood under a formaldehyde sky. The city and its sundered justifications moved by like a dream. Rain hammering the chassis. Here and there were crushed cars apparently sucked into the asphalt. What doesn't kill you leaves you exhausted.

I used the Mantarosa's denial-allow cloak for camouflage, detecting and projecting whatever onlookers were not willing to acknowledge - but these days people were disbelieving enough at the sight of a functioning vehicle. The propulsion system was spun by state-differential energy. It depended on geographical time zones, taking advantage of the nano-difference in time between the vehicle's hood and trunk. The contradictional friction was small but absolutely constant, even while the car was stationary - some houses had been powered the same way.

I parked up outside the Delayed Reaction Bar and sunk a pneumatic anchor spike to a depth of eight feet. The little gyroscopic context engine whirred to a stop and the Mantarosa clammed shut behind me as I made the sign of the Errorverse and entered the bar.

The atmosphere was one of lethal chemistry and vaporized intent. The ceiling was haemorrhaging; the floor magnifying submerged tiles like the poison scales of a dragon. It was raining in my kidneys. The walls were dark brown like burnt sugar and on one hung a pug clock giving only the vaguest suggestion of time. When I drew near to anyone I could hear the muted death of braincells like popping candy.

The barman Don Toto was a bald fellow with all the usual eyes and noses assigned where they might do the least harm. But Toto was smart, a researcher. He had discovered a crime between assault and grievous injury and taken out a copyright. Today most of his body was taped over with bandages. He could barely walk and perhaps didn't want to.

He was playing the bar like a keyboard.

'Antifreeze, with everything.'

'Taffy Atom, my hypergora friend. You look like a million dollars that rightfully belong to someone else.'

'Really?'

'No. You look like a wishbone in a coat.'

'Thanks, Toto. You fill a bastard-shaped hole in my life. I see your clientele are still those whose philosophy arrives by chute and leaves by trashcan.'

Behind me I heard the strop of a gun being unsheathed and Toto perked up: 'Ignore him, gentlemen, his heart has a rat's tail, it's horrible. His body makes powerful appeals to the earthworm and other crawlites, with no help from you.'

I looked cautiously behind me to see the offended drinker give it the thousand yard sneer and sheath his flaw. He returned to reading *Modern Hernia* magazine.

Toto leaned and spoke more quietly. 'Where you been the last ten years, Atom?'

'A part of the world you can still see the face of the planet, Toto.'

'Whatcha been up to?'

'Evolving. It's the latest thing - and always is. What's been happening over here?'

He told me. Kids were using old memory sticks for ammo. For a while there was a fashion for specially-made throwing stars in the shape of letters. The name of Allah was favoured by beginners, having the compensatory four blades of a good razor. Sanskrit was intermediary and Kabbalic figures were blunt enough to demand the strength and skill of a master, some favouring whole word symbols such as Yud Yud Lamed (Letting Go). Betty had been the mob since Cortez the Killer went mad and ate his own ass. His death and illegal conversion to rotten meat had been the talk of the town. All Cortez's boys went over to Betty. 'Her fort's charm central. Waited long enough.'

'Betty's steady. Repair this drink, it's broken.' Toto repaired the freeze. 'Your answers are partly obscured by bandages, I notice. Brotherhood again?'

'Galoot,' Toto replied. 'Asked after you, strangely enough.'

'Fella with a doughy head and a show pistol?'

'Yeah, fronted-up. But he used the muscles of his upper body for the attack. It was a game of pure opposition. He broke my arm, and my other arm - and my other arm. That third arm might have been my leg.'

'Both arms and a leg.'

'And my other leg.'

'I see.'

'And my other leg.'

'Now I'm confused, Don Toto.'

'Not half as confused as I was. I told him where your old office was but I was sure you was still outta town.'

'No-one could know I was coming in.'

Don Toto began to speak about self-similarity in regard to time when regarded as a single item, but my mind was wandering, trying to correlate. Everything has been deemed illegal - so, which crime to select? Pick any point along an infinite series. None can be 'wrong'. Beerlight was like most cities in that fear was the master builder. For the average person there was no way to die here that was not dangerous, inconvenient, or both.

A fly was ticking against a tube light.

'My gun's missing, Toto.'

'Damn silly thing to say aloud.'

'It should have been behind my office.'

'You could hotwire a guzzler.'

'Nah. Parker still in business?'

The gunsmith and hitman Brute Parker was renowned for having such control over his ammo he could shoot people in a 'beguiling' way. Classically-trained in grudgecraft.

'More a religion with him now. Find him in the Square pretty often, at prayer. Keeps his gun in a cage and the key in a holster. The holster is strapped around the waist of an ape.'

'Let me guess. The ape is in the cage and he is the ape.'

'This describes us all, Atom.'

'Very droll.'

'Here's one you won't get - a paradox. "A" states that everything "B" says is a lie. "B" states that everything "A" says is true.'

'Easy. A and B are lying and mistaken, both and simultaneously. Happens all the time.'

'Okay,' he frowned, thinking, then brightened. 'How about this one. I want power in desperation, but when comfortable I am content with comfort. Who am I?' His look was calculating.

I realised I didn't know, and became brisk. 'What a one you are for questions, Toto. Well, I better go check in somewhere, the Socket maybe.'

'What about the slabhead who's been asking for you?'

'Unless you got any better ideas, which no-one expects, I'll consult the gap and see if there's any pattern.'

'They'll be cutting your clothes off before you're finished.'

'Thanks, Toto.'

I drove to the Eyesocket Hotel on Devant Street and took a room. On the bed was a brown beetle the size of a violin. I flipped a sheet over it and threw the whole sack out the window, laying down.

'ibeam. Give me an exploded view of this argument.'
I repeated Toto's 'power in desperation' taunt and
a wireframe hovered below the ceiling. The shape
broke open and revolved, its elements re-assem-
bling in a different shape - now the structure gave
off a more electric flavour. 'The average citizen,' I
concluded. Toto would have been gratified to know
I'd resorted to tech to solve the puzzle. I'd have to
think one up for him.

I switched to the gap. The gap factors in the
peripheral vision around the edge of the net - on
the principle that the real facts were sunk in the
gaps and brackets of the equation, like the sparkle
of light between leaves. The net had more holes
since its collapse and slow rebuild. From these
patterns of absence I inferred the extent of the city's
onrush. It was pretty precise. The gestalt was an
irregular cylinder dried open at both ends, with an
entropic wind fluming through it. People clung to
the inside walls like dead flies. I was amazed that
any dynamic could be maintained here. Was it pure
after-momentum or was it actively pushing toward
something? Was any new energy being created in
this husk? It looked totally played out. Science had
changed the point at which a thing was declared
dead, but that presupposed an outside observer
who could call time. And I was getting involved.
The truth is, I was so cheerful to be saying a final
goodbye I got generous with my time - a gem of a
mistake. I'd fallen through a hole in my head.

*Get out, Atom. Look at the shape of the thing, it's
a bonanza of emptiness. You owe it nothing.*

There should be a procedure to formally quit a
species.

I got up and stood at the window, which showed an edge of the O from the dead neon HOTEL on the front of the building. In the street below, a car lay smoking on its side. The crump of distant explosions became hypnotic. My pupils were poised to dilate but never got the chance - there was a landphone like a landcrab on the sidetable and this shrilled into life. It was Toto. 'You get the answer to that riddle yet?'

'Sure. Comfort's the one merit of material empires.'

'So where is it now, eh? End of empire. Cloudy remains found by robot submarine etc.'

'A casino under murky water, roulette wheel locked up with moss.'

'Beautiful. Anyway, why I called - there's an event node at the Stina Gate.'

'Sounds promising.'

'Promising? You searched the gap, right? And you don't get this? You're outta touch, Atom.'

I switched the receiver from my right hand to my left. 'Guess I am.' It was strange. Even factoring in several flip-flops of irony the info didn't interest me - it seemed to have as much content as a decoy duck. I was still detuned. People de-cypher others' statements in the assumption that they don't mean what they say. The statements of someone who does mean what he says will also be put through the de-cyphering process - in other words, it'll be scrambled and nothing he tries to communicate will ever get across. Such a person can't even give secrets away. I've come to like this - I depend on it. But it plays merry hell in a fresh neighbourhood. 'You sure about this?'

'Let me reply with a question of my own.'

'No.'

As I put down the phone I gazed at the room safe. It was a single-use openless Chubb TriGuard with show relockers, anti-drilling plates, blast-resistant Trilite and Chobham armour - known in the trade as a 'trickledown'. I opened the bedside table. Inside was a copy of Eddie Gamete's *Haruspex Virus*. It hit me with the punctual surprise of being shot. An early example of Zero Point Literature, this book was like a device built for stress-testing prejudice and because such beliefs will buckle under an instant's examination, the remaining excess torque would tend to rip the reader open. It was a rehearsal for *The World Cup Ordination of Schottner Kier*, a later book that laid down the architecture of a linear accelerator in the reader's mind. This device was activated by a signal concept at the end of the text.

A little atmosphere cradled exquisite minutes in which I contemplated the first few pages. Some of it was pretty straight:

'As the police, the thieves and their authorities work to the detriment of the majority, all the majority do is applaud. Now, ofcourse, too few are left alive to get a real applause going. Maybe a timid little patter now and again. But the approval is still there. Approval keeps the spine straight and the chin up, in a slave.'

Then I closed the book and left the hotel, stuffed to the eyes with questions.

3

RING THE BELLS, I'M GOING OUT

Parked by the shamefaced and abandoned building of the Terminal Embassy, I nursed a needle, thumb on the plunger. It was Jade, the stuff people took to either raise or lower their intelligence to a median level: communication was almost impossible otherwise. Tonight though, a mistake.

If your heart stops in Beerlight they steal the wheels off it. I cloaked the car and walked down Plenti Street in slate Faraday pants, a decoy shirt and glacier glasses rare as copper wire. Stina Hang was a smashed piazza of shattered asphalt and white dust. The bone idle stood around traditional trashcan fires or sat on the lumpy ground trying to identify their next meal. I spotted a group of three guys who looked to be Mexican. They were sat around a fire, smoking cigars rolled on the thighs of baffled women. I let them know I was coming by giving a brief sketch of my interests and depravities:

'My hobbies are shaped charge explosions and being meticulously misunderstood. Other than that I'm as useless as a hen on a garbage island.'

'Friend or foe?' asked the leader, a dashing bastard in a vintage AV-6 flight jacket.

'Neither.'

'Join my bottle.'

I did as instructed. 'Here I am, crouched for adventure.' I found I had to shout above the sound of growing mustaches. 'Mexican eh?'

'*Si* - it's final.'

I drank whisky out of a dead spyglass.

He continued in a sawmill voice. 'I first came to Beerlight on a sniper exchange program, to see the Miracle of the Snarling Virgin. What I found dried the slime on my heart. Numb calibrations. Russian doll pinatas. Abominations.'

I nodded. That sounded like the way it might have happened. 'I agree tooth and nail. I remember when there were banks to be robbed or supported. Let's pray something'll crawl out of an ocean trench to bring retribution on us all, eh? I'll drink to that! I'll die, and nature will probably be unsatisfied with rotting me once.'

'As for me, my judge shall find me ready and ripe with crimes.'

'We'll be clearing you away with a leaf-blower.'

'As we are now being frank, whose eyes nest behind them blockers, senor?'

I took inventory before replying. They were all multistrapped but I could only see a few of their flaws. The speaker was dressed in brown, with yellow gloves. He had a Stigmata Hardball in an oxblood boast pocket and a few throwing knives in a waist sheath. The big guy was a bullet-banded jack of clubs - he was stroking a Kingmaker pistol like a pet and had something that might have been a Failsafe bar in a shoulder rig. The third guy appeared to be playing air-dagger. He had hair the appearance and cost of tobacco and an irregular object in the centre of his face. I could only explain it as some sort of nostril array. He favoured a Calico mini sub with a helical magazine. It was unlikely any of them had sidespace holsters.

'The name's Atom.'

Telling him this was like interrupting a Kamikaze pilot as he straps on his alice band. He frowned, making a notch between his eyes like a trigger guard. 'You and your bloodcurdling calm are well known to me. Gumshoe analog. Gun in cookie jar etc. Thought you were dead.'

'Sure, dead like a fox.'

'They say you have blank hands and that you killed a President with the one and only Siri gun.'

'Unavoidable I'm afraid,' I said, pursuing a course of mildness with utmost resolution.

He thought that over without reaching any apparent conclusion. Then he smiled benignly. 'As to that, this round man is Jose,' he said, indicating the bewigged guy with the knife. 'This rocklike man is Junco, known as *El Mozote*.' That was the squarejaw jack with the chest fence and heavy sender. 'And I am Alfonso.' He gave a ghastly grin.

'Well, now I can put names to faces.'

He looked as if he were tasting his own teeth. 'Ach, you strike a nerve. Look at Jose's face. There's not one feature you can name with any certainty. He looks like he began as a man and then Mother

Nature lost her nerve. Nose like a chicken bone and downhill from there. And *El Mozote* - his face, apparently through the workings of sheer chance, has gathered into this pattern while standing fast against the eroding forces of the sea. I make no great claims for mine either. It is just a nose surrounded by other features that swirl around for lack of clear instruction.'

'Well, if we're comparing, how about my own face - fixed-wing ears, a snap-brim forehead and forty-calibre tearducts.' I indicated Jose's legs. 'What manner of things are these?'

'His legs. And now you know everything. Ach, look at their faces. And look at yours. And mine.'

'How long would that be fun? No, gentlemen, I think it's time we admitted we've sealed our fates by being born behind these distortions.'

We continued the small-talk, air phrases melting before they were received, and touched lightly on politics, agreeing that several well-known figures should be destroyed.

Alfonso ritually offered up the old story of Roni Loveless, the boxer who, ordered to throw a fight, beat not only his opponent but everyone in the arena and its locality in an outward-blooming explosion of violence against enforced mediocrity. Protocol demanded I counter, so I laid out the story of the guy who had quietly killed and disposed of a delegation of government agents visiting his home in Atlanta. A follow-up posse sent to investigate were also quietly disappeared. A subsequent arrest crew were soon missing in action. Word got out and hundreds, then thousands of people flocked to his door seeking a way out. The address was eventually posited as a means of population control. Maybe this last was only legend. My audience sat thoughtfully around the mothering pot.

I was silent for a while, idly painspotting. A moon covered in vaccination scars had ignited Beerlight's cordite borealis, forming concentric rings of death-smoke. Winged spiders with loose legs wove feebly around in the air. Stina Gate itself was like the gate in *King Kong* but without the tiki styling. Old code graffiti covered the dented metal behind which stretched a desert consisting not of sand particles but of those sleep-crumbs people roll out of their eyes - the baked flats of the Fadlands. This gap in the world was the endplace of a culture pumping nothingness into a chick-mouthed vacuum. It was artificial, this absence - I knew the difference between it and the tilted fertility exposed when a civilisation is scored back to its bedrock of illusion and doom. There was something honest about the latter's unrealistic hope. The Fadlands were about cowardice, the denial of anything intense or specific. It had spread like a stain without detail, a blandness its inhabitants had subdivided to keep themselves busy.

Stina Gate was not the portal for contraband notions.

'What was the man's name, senor.'

'Which man?'

'The man in Atlanta who disappeared the killers.'

'I don't remember.'

Like a police statement, why did it seem more unlikely once it was said? Because something couldn't be defined as a lie until it was stated aloud.

'Why did he do it?'

'Well, the term "altruism" springs to mind. You familiar with it? European folk tales are full of this sort of thing, where someone will do something for no visible reason.'

Apparently I wasn't supposed to know the answer, so when I supplied it I was surprised by the outbreak of evasive fronting-off it provoked. I was still evaluating normalcy here and seeking a baseline in case I decided to comply.

I was worried the Jade had slowed my reflexes, so I popped the pin off a pocket time cap, putting a three-second gain on my existence - I was three seconds into their future. If necessary I would fake a response delay.

'What's in the cooking pot?'

'Know them for what they are: beans. You want?'

'No, thanks.' If he'd handed me the ladle it would have gone out of time-phase and given the game away.

'True. Our short acquaintance ought not to be themed around beans. Never trouble anyone else with what you can hate fully yourself, eh?'

I was starting to think he had a point when a movement at the Gate drew my eye. The Gate slowly opened a crack, allowing through a couple of ragged figures in a puff of dust. A door of those proportions should be approached with a frown of survival. But the kid possessed the sort of face that looked as if it had just that instant run out of ideas. He stood there with no method or disguise, his shapeless kecks flapping up a storm. Next to him an old man with a sharkskin face was wearing a jellycoat flushing from cyan to orange to purple.

I didn't remark on them, and they were almost

out of the plaza when Jose noticed them with a start. Without even standing he pulled a stained-glass grenade from somewhere and pulled the pin, throwing it over-arm at the retreating figures. The air around them scrambled and they blipped out of sight. It was a chronobomb.

Jose explained the situation to the others while betraying no anxiety. They responded likewise, and the three began unhurriedly to check and load their weapons, lumbering to their feet and stretching. They turned their attention to the Gate. The corroded doors were shut. For one who had been so ferociously open about his shortcomings and those of his gang, Alfonso was a confident guy.

Everyone had set to sharpening their spare keys since America went full-scarcity, and the philosopher Merk Duidelijkop had devised an extensive measurement system of dismay, the Merk Scale, which escalated through 32 million increments. Over the next twenty minutes I watched the three Mexicans climb this scale until they were in a state of savage melancholy. They had sat back down, and were looking angrily at the closed Gate. Their time bomb was mis-firing, maybe. My little delay switch wasn't strong enough to intersect. Depending on the wiring it could have been a simple expiation misfire. I'd have to ask Maddy later on.

'This is getting a little creepy now, Alfonso. I like it.'

He seemed not to hear, smoking a shock absorber.

'You should try nicotine patches.'

He looked at me with indignation. 'Patches? We

don't need no stinkin' *patches!*'

Their gruff malaise continued, with Alfonso throwing me increasingly suspicious looks.

'Yes, I've done everything wrong, as usual,' I said, playing with the smashed blacktop as if I were on a beach. 'Yep, that's the desiccated tarantula in the coconut. Wisdom is something grown, not arranged, buckaroo.'

'Don't call me buckaroo, Senor Atom. It would be a simple matter to let a bullet escape in your direction.'

'Oh I suppose mine is the sort of tap-water truth that's taken for granted. The pattern of our shifting cowardices has a meaning. I'd like to build you an amazing scale model. And now I begin.'

This unbridled indifference seemed to annoy them. Alfonso gestured at Junco. 'The Thistle here, his personality basically consists of compressed air. He believes that every talent must unfold itself ultimately in bloody violence. Like this.' And he snapped his fist at the air, knocking a fly briefly off-course.

At the same moment, Junco thought it wouldn't be a bad idea to fire the Kingmaker at me. I stepped aside. Junco looked blankly confused. Aiming at my past, he had seen the bullet go through me.

'Whatever you think you know about being Mexican comes from me,' I announced. I don't know why I said it - I blame the drugs - but I was still laughing when Jose sapped me over the head. When I hit the ground my face was positioned to complete the sentence 'Belting the old noggin eh?' so it hit the dirt chin-first, digging in like a trowel. They had a lot of trouble moving me, apparently.

4

FIFTY-FIFTY CLOWN

I was dreaming about a grand cathedral of sea cucumbers belching sediment through the windows. I missed my wife.

I awoke leaking into a strange room. I was strapped to an old self-surgery seat. My shirt had already died. The stainless steel throne stood in a garage littered with car batteries, syringes, crumbs of glass and scattered gaskets. There was a pile of tyre-rims like cybernetic haloes.

It sounds more fun than it was. The moment fell into me like painful rain. The Jade and time cap had worn off. I was blood-sick, time-sick. I rolled my head a little - my neck felt granular. It seemed my throat had been doing some wholesale rasping. Three fingers were missing from my left hand, leaving the thumb and index.

They weren't too bright - they'd left me both trigger fingers.

Wearing his hair back to front, Jose stood at the lowered garage door in some sort of apron. And there was Alfonso, sitting sadly on a pile of galvanised steel tubes and looking as if he might cry all over his Astra jacket. They seemed in worse shape than me, as ragged as if they had been keeping up a show of goodwill. Maybe I'd already been annoying them - but I didn't remember. I supposed I'd been running interference and then wiped that part of my brain before re-emerging. I had no option but to start from the beginning.

'The sun has risen, senor,' Alfonso said, perking up a little. 'The brotherhood have the streets.'

Jose approached me with a cordless hammer drill. 'Coffin bugs know the geometry of disappearance, Senor Atom. They will explain it to you soon.'

He proceeded to demonstrate what he called 'the sawmill essentials' of persuasion with various expert shoves, workshop horrors and other morale-blasting monkeyshines. It was like a sort of electric birthday, and seemed designed to provoke me into a reckless and unguarded outburst. I didn't think of many remarks, except the unvoiced one that they didn't go nearly far enough. As it was I seemed to horrify them every time I opened my mouth - even when I asked explicitly after the relevant protocol.

But they were enlivened. The project interested them so much that they frequently stared at me to see if I was starting to like it too. Jose referred to his knife as 'the key to your throat'. I realised these people would quickly exhaust me with their enthusiasm.

'Your friend waiting to welcome your guests at the Stina?'

They looked annoyed, which meant the kid and the old man hadn't entered the city again yet. Alfonso stood and began punching me almost as if it mattered to him personally. I was surprised - baffled, really - at this level of insecurity. Like most interrogators, they were trying to act cool but something was bugging them. Their position forced them to admit there was something they lacked. Ironically this imbalance will tend to have a fella making one wild claim after another to set them at their ease. As they continued sawing out the rungs of my skeleton I was at a loss as to what else I could do to soothe these bastards. My rotten reassurances left them apparently inconsolable. Jose threw part of my explanation back at me - it sounded strange cut out that way, without top or tail, so I added some new words at the front and back, and he punched me in the nose. Then with a brittle quiver of childlike petulance he started smacking my head about like a tetherball.

It wasn't really a matter of throwing a scare into me but of discouraging me until I indicated that I understood things the same way they did. Though it was hard work and paid nothing, it would have been unworthy of me to regret or criticise any of us.

An interrogation is not just a form of emotional feasting, it's really a form of divination. Its arcane conditions are supposed to conjure information that none of those taking part actually know. A setup designed to expect deception will tend to generate it, bending information into 'true' by forced surmise.

Everyone comes out ahead. On this occasion the principle players' self-delusions - theirs and mine - were soon mixed and intermingled. Their conjecture was exhaustive and my groans were without content. Of course, my knowing nothing resulted in information moving osmotically in the opposite direction. Their central theme was the Heber kid and my connection to him. They talked about him as if the matter were too familiar to merit much detail, but I gathered that he was a military intelligence asset. Meanwhile they were waiting for enlightenment while obviously afraid of what they might discover. We seemed to be at crossed-purposes.

At least they were uncertain, not bored. But finally they did seem bored. The general sentiment seemed to be that they'd wasted enough time already and here they were. They became reproachful and morose. Alfonso's face looked like a cow's. This despair of theirs led me to seek some kind of consolation for them. I evinced stubborn dignity, dazzling indifference, mimsy flirtatiousness, hard-earned sagacity and enigmatic radiance, all in an effort to keep them entertained. Jose looked at me in pained wonder, then became indignant. Alfonso seemed overcome with disbelief and pity, adding a rosy grace note to this depressing shambles of an interrogation.

'Maybe we're going at this wrong,' I said. 'You're not allowing me much latitude - not enough for truth, anyway. I can't believe you really want to know, and apparently I've nothing more to learn from you. So why don't we abandon the project as a failure?'

I was feverish, but I think I made a pretty good case for my remaining meat being of less use than the bits they had claimed so far. I would sooner yield to the micro-banditry of ageing than their surgical persuasions. It was a solid argument. Only the terminally suspicious would assume it came with an agenda.

They looked disappointed.

'D'you think I'm *made* of blood?'

'Come now, you've got more than you give yourself credit for,' said Alfonso.

I succumbed. 'That's it. This interrogation sucks. It's the worst one I've ever been in. You guys don't know what the hell you're doing. And that's the one thing you didn't count on. You've cheapened a beautiful evening with the torture theme. I didn't think you were scared enough to need this much chair.' I did not keep from them the fact that they appalled me and that their end could be traced within the stained fringe of any horizon.

Jose breathed hard but didn't say anything. He looked genuinely hurt. This sudden gravity seemed to mature him.

'What was the man's name, senor,' Alfonso asked almost in a whisper, not looking at me and wandering way off the point. 'The man in Atlanta who disappeared the killers.'

He clutched at his stomach, vaguely puzzled. Then he folded down hinge by hinge, finally slapping his face to the floor.

I recognised the motion immediately - someone had just discharged a Bohr gun through the wall. A Bohr worked via quantum entanglement, using the particles of the loaded bullet to activate those of its entangled partner in the victim. The loaded bullet was ejected after the operation, as re-firing would only re-install the same quantum bullet in the same impact position.

Jose was up and at the metal wall of the garage door, drawing the Calico while at the same time activating what looked like a counterwave belt studded with vortex coils - the Bohr gun wouldn't harm him. A rectangle of light appeared at his side - an inset door had opened in the riser and Jose was instantly brawling with someone in front of it. The light flickered like a bulb battered and pinged by moths. I slipped the bloody left strap with my thinned left hand, releasing the right strap and attending to the leg fastenings as the small door fell closed and subfire flared in the gloom, smashing a fusebox. There was some ballistic commotion outside, the fusillade shifting gears back and forth in the signature syntax of the brotherhood. Apparently they were falling over themselves to shoot each other, or perhaps one other person who was unarmed. Jose threw his assailant aside and escaped through the small door. The gunfire changed register as the new element joined.

I staggered through tintacks and obtainium - the frayed view between my eyelashes revealed a woman with mustard-yellow hair, eyes the dead green of visa paper and a mouth that could tear out the sacred heart of Jesus. I confirmed the presence of a nose only much later. She was toting a Bohr 5.56mm rifle and slung under her purple leather coat was a hardshell shotgun, at a minimum. She'd probably weigh no more than 80 pounds drenched in blood. 'Lux Murphy - FBI.'

'Good - I need drugs.'

The garage door was lifting like a curtain before a stage.

5

VERSUS

We stood before the swelling rectangle until the door grated into place above us. All I could see at first was a collision of dustclouds, and then the dim skeletons of cars. Shell-track was underlining lengths of air as someone begot bullets into the atmosphere. In fact the shifting time-values attested to a galore of factions. Whether a bullet is a particle or a wave depends on your observation - head-on or as a bystander. Some of the slugs were pinging around in here.

We ran into the fanfare of gunfire, past a crushed yellow cab that lay on its roof. It had cracked like an egg but hadn't been stripped yet. We scrambled into an old crater, testament to the end of a bomb-zombie whose final act had trenched the street. Weeds now fringed the suicide's ground zero and I peered over this into the airborne dust.

I could tell that aside from a few preliminary

outrages the battle hadn't really kicked off. These public quarrels involving the brotherhood were open to everyone. Jose was somewhere, I could hear his Calico. There were also some kids who had probably been out playing real murder ARGs. Bullets were the only vitamin source they ever ingested and they'd react to injuries like a sugar high. For good measure a rogue sentient gunhead sprinted and rattled about like a toy crane, propelled by impulses that synchronised with the skirmish by dumb coincidence.

Prowler light-bars were pulsing in the smoke. The brotherhood - active ignorance in its cleanest form. It was many years since they had felt the need to give a motive for an arrest. Like the behaviour of their suspects, it was assumed to be instinctive and innate. After all the recent collapses the cops had found themselves strangely denuded. They had proved too backward to be employable for manual labour; were declared too careless and forgetful to plant seeds and too aggressive even to stand sentry. So there was an unspoken agreement that they should carry on as before, supervising the carnage at large.

They hit one of the kids and the pieces of her hung apart, flopping wet to the sidewalk. The smoke cleared a little and there he was, in eye-popping 3D: Chief Blince, the man primarily responsible for depicting law enforcement in Beerlight city. Seniority by sheer biomass. His philosophy was the most complete fossil of its kind ever found. I could have sworn I saw a gravitational tide around him, the hidden physics of hypocrisy, its sickly scaffolding shoring up his bulk. He raised a bullhorn. 'I'm having a lotta fun over here, nearly more than I can handle. Sure you don't wanna join me? Even the coldest among you gotta feel tempted. Use of deadly force is authorised, as usual. Nuns, bargain-hunters, unbiased observers - I've damaged them all.' He talked a little more but that was the gist of it. The ballistic charm escalated, echoes slapping back between the stale, half-eaten buildings.

The Fed girl rolled over, handing me a rifle whose architecture was densely ornamented with crazy golden scrollwork and other ceremonial lavishness. I wasn't new to exotic ordnance but I'd never seen anything like it. It looked like a gun built by Aztecs. The body was zoom-flake pineapple gold upholstered in burgundy leather round the stock and fore-end.

'You want me to...'

'You're ready to do more than that.'

I'd dismissed it as a coffee table gun but under all the translucent tortoiseshell it looked to be a rail cannon, its barrel the width of a toilet-paper tube. I test-fired a single shot that left the flared bellmouth with no more sound than a snapping icicle. Such experiments always aroused opposition or the pretence of it in the hope of profit, and I could see the cops perking up. Through the telescopic sight I watched them dart this way and that amid their roadblock, under a sky ulcerated with clouds. I knew at last where we were - I could see behind them the bruise-blue silhouette of Olympus Dump. I pressed the firing stud on repeat-fire, the volley sounding like the flurring of a tight deck of cards. Later I learned the gun was smartened, the rails charged with contrary accelerant powered by the victim's preference to live. That so many of the shots smacked the dirt well short of the blockade was due more to the cops' despair than my rusty aim. But enough hit home, stitching armour and popping cherry lights. Glass exploded into a surf of jumping pearls. Three cops went down, two by ricochet, I think. Many evinced surprise, though they would have been baffled if their gunfire were not reciprocated.

Recoil is like hearing your own accent. I hadn't fired a gun in seven years and it felt like someone had punched me in the shoulder. I'd forgotten, it was a real workout.

Guns started snapping off all over, unexacting but lively. Jose came out of nowhere, trotting to a crouching halt behind the crinkled snout of the flipped cab. He wasn't our ally but of course he was versus the cops so he was happy to hunker nearby on our right but at a slight angle. The ARG kids were on our left behind a fallen gun shop billboard, also at a slight angle that satisfied their independence. Ideally a complete circle would allow for everyone. Without the cops, our three emplacements could close to a triangle. The crappiest arrangement would be a square. Why? I pictured a conflict fractal, the same patterns repeated at every scale.

The girl Murphy had switched to a Kratos triage rifle, blasting monochrome judex ammo that hit quite low in the overall composition. A grenade went off and the debris sprayed forward. The little pop-spanner lost its head and stood still, motivations forgotten. A kid skidded forty feet before rolling loosely to rest, and the cops had a field day emptying bullets into the already lifeless and boring body.

These shots and explosions inevitably seemed mere frivolities to those not involved in our dispute, and several passers-by stopped to corrugate their foreheads in our direction. One in particular also held up a dog, its frowning face next to his own doubling the sentiment of puzzled disapproval. It was a great bit of work and I started laughing. But when I shouted at the Fed girl to look at the dog I found I was pointing at empty air, the passers-by having satisfied their curiosity and moved on. My voice petered out even as I vouched for the dog's dependability. I couldn't blame Murphy for her look of disbelief.

'Give yourselves up,' bellowed Blince through the loudhailer, 'if you dare.' I could tell he was barely paying attention. Rather than moving upward in his career he was swelling without any special direction. 'I conquered my fear of betrayal, so can you. Surrender at the nearest and dearest opportunity and we'll extend you every courtesy, up to and including arbitrary blame and exquisite violence.'

'Hardly a novel danger,' I shouted. I was getting into the swing of things. Someone else asked what securities they were offering by way of guarantee. This was met with the traditional silence from the brotherhood and the ballistic exchange continued.

Everyone was up and at it, running around and enjoying themselves. The triage fire was barely dividing, heading straight for the roadblock. The cops hurled curses at us for finding fault with them, yet they were the first to suggest that we throw down our own weapons. They complained that we had offered them no payment and we countered that they should therefore not be here. It was the old argument backed by the grand old wall of fire. Nothing was too rich or precise for it. Did it feel forced? Maybe I was projecting.

Jose didn't help. He had switched to single-shot and was firing in a contrary style that was only heightened by his obvious self-satisfaction. For a while he scuttled several feet backward with every shot, as if mirroring the bullet's trajectory. Then he would shout a word inaudibly at the same instant he fired, so that even the finest marksmen felt they were missing something. Finally his encouraging cry of 'Go!' just after shooting, supplanted by his peering through an opera glass to spectate the bullet's progress, created in everyone a sense of dismal failure and boredom.

A burning squadcar peeled off, snapping over the headless free gun and fishtailing from side to side. Then it slowed to a stop, the driver emerging to roll around and beat at the flames, or perhaps he was energetically waving his arms and legs to communicate something he'd realised amid this extremity. Several kids shot at him, not with the wholehearted delight one would expect but with a grim maturity, as though it was a duty. I jerked my head around at a sharp explosion. Jose was replaced where he stood by a cloud of blood. Blince was firing a Hardballer while stuffing his face with a submarine sandwich.

My rail gun flurred on empty. Murphy tapped me on the arm and I saw she was priming some sort of goop unit. She pitched it and we ran. The muscle grenade expanded, ramming the street with meat. The undifferentiated tissue began dissolving almost immediately, but it was enough to clog everyone in position for several moments. We quickly left the messy series of reprimands and counter-reprimands behind us.

We found the Mantarosa and I opened a pint screen in the dash. Madison Drowner frowned out. 'Why don't you come through?'

'Got company - coker.'

'Fed?'

'And the Hand's missing from the recharging well. I need your help on launch windows for a timebomb.'

'Pipe or sphere?'

'Sphere.'

'Transparent kinda like a powerball?'

'More metallic colours like a Christmas decoration, but faceted.'

'It's probably a Vanzetti LPR - localised progress reset device. There are three default settings: ten minutes, ten hours, 24 hours. You look like hell.'

I peered in a wing-mirror - my face was bruised purple black across the middle, like there was a vulture flying out of my eyeline. My hair was spiky with dried blood. 'Colour me damaged, babe. Back soon.'

'See that you are.'

I popped the beak of the car to free the swan unit. Folded down to the size of a toy harp, it was like an obstetric sculpture in white plastic. 'Wake up,' I whispered, and the swan unfolded itself wing by wing, tilting to stand, and raising its head last.

Its eyes blinked on. It looked cute. I grabbed its face by some jowls which extended automatically for just such occasions. 'You crazy swan,' I cried, tugging the jowls. 'You crazy swan! I love ya!'

'Don't do that,' said the swan.

'You crazy swan! Anyways, I need you to look out for new arrivals at the Stina Gate.'

The swan hopped away from me, waddled on the ground a little, and took off, flapping into an iron sky.

6

DO NOT STAND AT MY GRAVE AND WHOOP

At the hotel Murphy fixed herself an October Surprise and sat on a smashed TV whose innards looked like a city with kidney-coloured streets. I sat on the edge of the bed and opened a can of water. My left hand felt like a wedge of poison sticks. I'd wrapped it in a strip of rotten curtain patterned with brown roses.

The beating was enough to prompt me to put everything else aside and deal with the pain. 'I think my eye's blown.'

'Lose much blood?'

'I've got DNA base pairs I haven't even used yet. That was nice of you to haul my chestnuts out of the blaze back there. Kind of a miracle.'

'So's bleeding upwards.'

'Was I doing that again? They seemed determined to find me mistaken. Their ancient form of wonder-working depends on it. Pretending you're not helpless is just a coping strategy. I would have died for nothing.'

'All do.'

I lit a shock absorber. My alertness was for her sake - as was the fact that I was awake at all.

'As for the broken nose, I've decided to take it as a distinction - one of many bad decisions in my life. How'd you find me?'

'Hole in the gap. You reversed into the story like a Florida gran, Atom. What's the connective tissue?'

'No mystery there. A slabhead warned me off the kid so I got serious. Then I found the Mexicans fiending for him at the Gate. They screwed up with a chronobomb. I've seen better timing from a stuffed olive. But the banditos caught me off-balance - I've been out of town a long time. There seems to be way less torque under the hood these days, but maybe I haven't connected enough to feel it yet.'

'Fed training says the most dangerous town is one where the advent of crime is very recent and its novelty keeps everyone wasteful and imprecise, thinking they're proving something. I don't think there are any towns like that anymore. Why'd you leave?'

'I figured out what the cops were doing right. But when I incorporated the lesson, they didn't care for it. Now I get back and find Cortez is growing human in the ground.'

She smiled. 'Yup. Neon headstone, flashing arrow pointing jauntily down. Casket with a half-lid, the works. Inscription says "This Tombstone is Not a Toy." I guess there's justice if you dig deep enough in a graveyard.'

'No, that's just forgetting.' I dragged on the shocker. 'Well, you've given me no cause to doubt you're human, at least. How long you been here?'

'When bad things happen to good people.'

'Always? Thought you were from out of town.'

She humphed. 'I got assigned right here on the seamy side of life.'

'It's the seams that hold it together.'

'What I kept telling them. They interpreted it as dud loyalty tuning. Got a burn notice from the ruin.'

'Can they afford to burn anyone these days?'

'There was some knock-on when the Pentagon went up five years ago. Thank god the populace hadn't the balls to take over even when there was a corpse at the wheel.'

'When payback has atrophied for that long, it loses its spring.'

'But meanwhile years of my life were run under those wheels. I'd earned the wrong things, obviously. Even my compromises are in ruins. I want to live the sort of life that'll have consequences, Atom. A free agent.'

There was something in back of her explanation but I didn't know what it was. I watched the smoke pirouette upward from my gasper. 'Or maybe you're keeping their deals warm for them.'

She stood up and started moving with a sort of evasive aimlessness. She was a bullet of a girl, a design classic. Her weight would have doubled if she grew her hair. She lifted the cover of the Gamete book with the tip of a finger. 'What's the book about?'

'Amnesia conceals a killing, as usual,' I lied.

'Why does humanity always err to the boring,' she said, turning to me. 'To such extremes that it seems to want to be dead, or appear dead? Like an insect that looks like a dead twig so it's passed over by predators. Maybe humanity's instinctively doing the same, to be passed over by hostile aliens or something.'

I flashed on sacrificial spatial topology, the notion that the existence of a dense idea-space requires the sacrifice of a large adjacent near-vacuum. It was based on the unproven premise that there were a limited number of ideas and was fashionable because humanity wanted to believe that premise. 'Come on, we're too far along for that. Crappy's the default, so what.'

She stood close, looking into my face. Her hair solarised under the room's single lightbulb. But she smelt red as an aniseed ball. 'You're not like that, are you.'

It didn't seem like a question.

'I don't overlap. I'm old-fashioned.'

'I heard otherwise, lots.'

'Evolution, you mean.'

'What could be more old-fashioned?'

'Don't click on an empty gun. It's unattractive.'

She slapped me, twice. The first slap knocked the cigarette out of my mouth, the second put it back. 'I want to believe that,' I said. 'I really do.'

Someone was stumping sloppily up the hotel's bent stairs to our atrophied door. 'Doors come toward and around me without great effort on my part,' a voice rumbled from the other side. 'This much I know.'

Behind the warped wood hung a heart black as

an antique telephone. Blince was so fat he'd never heard it beating.

'Out the window,' the girl hissed. 'On the ledge.'

'You're making a simple deal very complicated,' I whispered, but I did as she said, sitting out of the window on to the flaked paint of the concrete ledge as Blince entered with a parrot key. I shuffled aside a little until I was within the O of the dead neon HOTEL. Night was creeping in and the air smelt of fresh sulphur. Behind me they were speaking, each smithereen to the other.

'Hands up,' said the chubby enforcer. 'Obvious, but it doesn't hurt to be reminded. Pivot, this is Lux Murphy, a Fed, such as they are. Murphy, you did the right thing calling me.'

'I didn't call you.'

'Then you're under arrest. Pivot, give her some cheese or whatever these things eat.'

Pivot sighed.

'And frisk her. Dollars to donuts she's flawed.'

'Let's both of us humour him, Miss Murphy,' said Pivot in a tone flat as a Cuban steak.

I watched the jagged distance of the skyline, the pinlight of guns firing like synapses across the city surface. A murder of squad cars was parked below, rooflights pulsing. It was summertime, I think. I looked to my wrist and remembered the beamer was gone.

Then the tangled noise of their speech continued. Pivot sounded indifferent.

'Girly gun with a joke grip. Ammo in her coat.'

'Gun used to be a heavy black oily concern like a carburetor,' Blince remarked. 'Now it's like a toy, looka this. What's it fire, mink-lined bullets? Entry wounds probably dotted with little hearts, I right?'

I hadn't seen Murphy stow the Bohr or the judex broom. She was good.

'This ammo's got a frog on the label. What kinda pills people firin' these days?'

'I was taught by my mother it was impolite to talk about one's ammunition.'

'You talk with the safety on. Kinda passive aggressive.'

'You wouldn't like the alternative.'

'Yeah? We saw you with Atom, grinning like a gash and firing a bigger piece than this. That's the stuff eh - bullets galore and cordite blowing up your pants leg. So what happened? It was all going dandy then you withdrew your participation.'

'It seemed to be doing you good.'

'You're like a spy in a colouring book aint ya Murphy? Cuter'n a glue-eyed baby sloth I reckon. What'd Atom do, give you a single longstem silencer? Watch out, he'll make a fridge magnet of your nose.'

'I'd like that.'

'Well, Murphy, ah, this isn't so good, this is looking pretty bad. You conspired with a known ... well, we better decide. What's his form, Pivot?'

Pivot, whoever the guy was, tapped at a handset. I heard my biography. Hours of legend were absent but some of it was true. Pivot's voice was diffident and dignified. 'His correlated intel jacket starts in mid-air. Nothing early on, no birth record, blank as Sanctus. Travelled under a false flag. Known aliases: Atman, The Malamatic, Man of the Blank Hands -'

'Acid dabs,' Blince commented.

'Probably. He's described as a *luftmenschen*, man of air, an interbeing, creature of absolute activity, lungs like a helicopter, living purely by his wits. He acknowledged no sanction or hierarchy.'

'Not unusual.'

'These days. But that stuff was still in play, back when the remark went in. His file is annotated with a considerable number of ideas and stupid drawings, such as this one of a pig watching a butterfly in a sunbeam - notice the pig has a placid smile on his face. Drives a Sarfatti Mantarosa with an anti-Blake motor.'

'The pig does the driving?'

'Atom, Chief. Got the skull of a smiley on the hood and some lightning. Portholes like a Thunderbird. He fits the four-point profile for a total bastard. Frequented the Fist of Irony and dated the Caere Twins. For a while he settled on a campaign of chakric sarcasm using a sleuth cover. There's this stuff about the stolen brain and the Presidential assassination, and Atom was interrogated. Claimed he was in Washington "visiting his rights". And the notes start getting quite strange later on. His mere face at the window not uncommonly leads to mayhem.'

For a moment I thought he'd seen me, but it was just words. Still, a wave of strangeness had drawn over me like polyester film. They knew more than I had realised. It seemed someone was quite taken with me and my successes. The vaunt song from inside had moved on.

'... with the backing of Madison Drowner who was nominally his armourer. The seventh difference is how light spilled out of the bloodstream. And even this jacket turns out to be a cypher describing various full-denial covert ops in perfect sequence.'

'But we compiled the jacket, pink-eye.'

'You bet. And I added to it after today's encounter. It resulted in three more pieces of classified information being found encoded into the files.'

'A real glory boy, eh?'

'Purportedly prophesied the Pentagon incident. Then he left town and there's nothing solid, just more of these speculations about the thirty-seventh nisterim. Now he's a blow-in.'

'So many moral and stylistic ambiguities. He seems to have spent his life stockpiling idiocies for us to scrutinize. Cuffing him'd be like putting a padlock on jello.'

'Saves himself from being a nonplussed innocent by having something always to do, anyway. This biography is unverifiable, obviously.'

'And a profanation of all we enjoy. All those years committing crimes, and never the same one twice. So you see, Murphy? If you cooperate in a broad general way, I can make the whole thing go away like nuclear sludge. As strange and counter-intuitive as it seems, I'm sworn to enforcing freedom. Witness the baleful charms of gravity upon a plummeting wretch as nature behaves like disaster's friend. See a seahorse smile, and then try to tell yourself you expected it.'

'I guess,' said Murphy, 'sometimes it helps to talk.'

'That's the stuff right there. Reality is discarded from the law like the marble chipped away to reveal a statue. That chipping away is my duty. Its performance requires certain aspects of the villain - in fact all of them, really, but tilted at a surer angle. As for justice, we just make a few jocular guesses and a lot of noise. No-one minds much.'

My headache had gone. I felt loose and relieved, as though my head had disappeared and I saw the world through two floating eyeballs. The night sky was an open secret.

A hooting noise to my right - the swan Strobe Talbot was tilting along the ledge toward me. Not much to look at, this white umbrella was the best urban smart drone manufactured by the Garuda Company. 'The targets are approaching the Gate,' he reported, and hopped on top of the O. He dropped a swingbar from his underside - I took hold with my good hand. Strobe blew his wings to full stretch and plunged us down Devant Street in a chronic manoeuvre that made me think, *My doom isn't stale after all.*

7

THE BATTLE OF STINA GATE

We skimmed over the warped grid of the city. They say a city is the detritus left over from a billion scams, but this was a city like broken bones, built too fast and dirty to be intentional. I was bleeding into it from the chemical pain at the end of my left arm. Then the old Trincado Tower swung by below and Stina Hang lifted at us like a diorama angled for display.

It looked to be in uproar, and I hadn't got there yet. Warning someone off is the most compelling way to inform them of an option, and sure enough a squadcar had set up in the plaza like a placard. Around it motives tangled like the tails of a king rat. It had the topological symmetry of what had yet to be learned. Dozens of parties were blasting refractive and prefig firearms across this congested arena. They were so frolicsome and serious I felt simultaneously sick and quickened.

The Gate was closing, the old man and the blonde teen crouching against it as it boomed into place. Junco had moved his vigil to a fire drum nearer to the Gate and was now pinned down, faced away from the Gate and firing everything he had. I flew right over him and let go of Strobe, dropping perfectly into the flaming trash can. My entry forced a gout of flames up around my body, making me wonder how other people did this and similar stuff with any enthusiasm. Why anyone would accept the obliteration offered by such a disappointing arrival was an even bigger mystery. I had overbalanced the drum onto the ground and now threw myself this way and that for a while, sometimes confronting onlookers in the process. And I found with a start that I was staring at the old man and the kid. For a moment they seemed scared of me, on account of my burning hair probably, and the particular way I was screaming. In fact I noticed that the firing had stopped as everyone watched this bewildering display.

When I had the fire out and sat breathing at the ground, the battle gradually stuttered back into play. My bloody paw had been cauterized, anyway. The kid and the old man had recovered and were now merely looking at me like dogs with nothing to lose. Heber was wearing a cheap suit like a kid at a wedding. It was battered and too small, and he hadn't even the sense to jettison the tie. He looked about seventeen. The old man was conspicuous in a defective chameleon coat that consistently flushed through with the opposite colour from its background. I pushed the pair into a crouch behind the fire drum.

Assault rifle charm and the swerving tracer wake of Kurras triage ammo crisscrossed the field of battle, illuminating a dimestore apocalypse. Seemed several parties had shown up wanting to do all their dying in one day, firing everything from rag-and-bone voodonics to Styx cannons to tat guns that fired embarrassing Mom tattoos. A chef was recklessly feeding an etheric belt through an old Vickers machine gun while giving out about this and that in a mixture of English, Behlta and Harangue. A mime in a half-car drawn by three lawyers was taking pot-shots with a Tuesday Afternoon Special. A frazzled clown brought down a nun with a flying tackle, and both instantly flared into a blot of dirty orange flame - one or the other must have been a bomb zombie. There was even an uncooked monkey scampering over the hardscrabble and busted blacktop. It seemed like every time I went into town, all hell broke loose.

The smaller detonations sounded like bad edits but a thermobaric shell blew open so close and loud I briefly forgot my current name. Through swirling smoke and particulates I saw something like a bandoliered picture card - Junco was holding a bulky strata gun showing several tiers of add-ons and no sign of its original identity. A Saab? He fired a salvo at the cop car, which seemed to go wide, and racked another shell into the gun's chamber. He tilted at an olive-drab Abrams tank covered in random insignia. A life lesson: tanks are faster than you think. This was speeding across the plaza until a vague auroral blackness peeled away behind it and it seemed to lose direction, plunging into a corrugated ammo hut. An eye-blinding fireball lit a group of roller-caged prowlcars as they took up position. Their deployment appeared incredibly unsophisticated, a staggered formation expressing an irregular equation with multiple values. Blince emerged from one into a speaker cage to spout unfathomable courtesies through a bullhorn. There was no pause in the charm bonanza and he had to holler above the blast of war. 'This is the police. None of us are remotely qualified to understand what is taking place here. Here's the crux of the nutshell - I propose a suspension of law until this outrageous state of affairs has been explained.'

I extrapolated nothing of interest from this and nobody took it more seriously than it deserved. Blince's mentality hadn't changed, though to me it seemed he was alone in not getting any thinner over the years. What with the current lack of new food supplies, I suspected an autopsy might find other people's bones in his body. Leon Wardial once argued that Blince shouldn't be allowed to live because gravitational force had infinite range. Blince continued, the cops to either side of him already firing trad and triage into the field.

'Now a word from the acting DA, Gordi Pivot, who has a warrant for search and seizure on your broken bodies. I'm proud to tell lies shoulder-to-shoulder with this man, whose jurisdictional fiend-ing would steal the wounds off a dead man.'

Blince signalled that this was all he knew or was willing to say by applying himself to the task of handing the bullhorn to Pivot and disappearing inside the armoured roller. Pivot was colourless, white-haired, an albino in cream. He took the bull-horn as he rose without enthusiasm or change of expression. 'Thank you Chief. I'm legally allowed not to understand what you're talking about, and you're legally required to support my position. Your own position within the law has clearly freed you from the necessities of common decency, and you are riding it bareback. This statement notwithstanding, I intend tonight to unspool the law's comic masterpiece, "disorder". In fact discord is not understood here as there is no condition with which to contrast it. But procedure must be fulfilled.'

The idea seemed to have no structure, only position and duration. Not that any crime-related arrest would occur here anyway: no money or barter had changed hands. Ammo darted away from the citizenry like rabbits released and again the cops reacted as if this mutuality was unforeseen.

Sheets of smoke rushed by wind revealed glimpses of cops locked in shame, craters smeared with matter and tagged with blossoms of fire, and dodging cage cars driven by jubilant kids. Flames balled skyward. Shots spanged off the fire drum, a recurring problem.

I'd got Strobe to signal the jalopy on the way over and now it was bumping over the fire-spotted moonscape toward me. Multiple onlookers made the car's cloaking muddled and flickery but most of them still managed to ignore it even after they'd bounced off the hood. When it pulled up I hauled the kid and the old man over and crammed them inside, being careful not to touch the scale gear.

Before I could climb in after them I saw another vehicle approaching. It was an old boilerplate truck once used to haul cannery water, and in the cab was the galoot who'd fronted off in my office. He seemed intent on flattening Junco. As the truck bore down on him *El Mozote* had ditched his shoulder cannon in my direction and was priming something that resembled a saw handle - I realised it was a Failsafe borderbar.

Before the breakup of states Johnny Failsafe had crossed numerous state borders to see if he could detect the subtle sensations of laws changing around his body - after all, laws were either real or they weren't. He had in fact found a microscopic transition point where no laws existed and extracted core-sheets for use as wall projections in clubs. But subsequent research had also revealed a small halting effect as one set of laws ceased and another set came into power. The momentary braking required to re-orient oneself had the same quality at every border, and by overlaying dozens of examples of this modality, technicians created an archetypal suprastate they termed 'whipped' - a condition in which the victim's progress is completely blocked by external decree. Now as the truck was about to smack him Junco stood with the borderbar in his left hand, took hold of it with his right and whipped it open like a chest expander. The truckfront crumpled like a beer can as it pounded to a stop, the rear lifting behind it as if the whole thing would flip ass-over-head.

Junco ducked out on the far side as the truck poised a while on its face like it was showing off a tricky headstand. In the cab the ape was fumbling to fire the same Birch gun he'd shown me in the office, but the Failsafe state backfired it. I couldn't tell if the galoot himself stopped because of the

Failsafe or because he was painted over the cab windows. The motor howling in frictionless outrage, the ancient machine finally went over, slamming to the ground and blocking the Gate closed. Junco seemed to have an epic skill set.

I salvaged his discarded stack cannon - what had seemed like a salvage title Saab actually looked to have been built around a barebook basic and massively elaborated with silver gridpulse hoops, ribbed ceramic cowling, a white shoulderbone grip that housed the gun's limbic system and bull bars like heavy sideburns. The pulse array tipped me that this was a firearm so powerful they advised you not to fire it without a helmet - a Permutation gun, which in an instant runs the victim's consciousness through every life state with the intelligence to collate its summation, as a result of which its victim chooses death.

At that moment a volley of cop triage fire diverged into five paths like jets at an airshow, then recombined and headed as one in my direction. It's difficult to think while lugging a gun the size of a scooter, but I aimed it into the air and fired off a blazing round, neutralising the triage ammo's criteria. They started twirling around randomly like fleas.

The Perm muzzle was fizzling, it shouldn't do that. It was weeping etheric accelerant. I dumped it in disgust and it lay smouldering like a jammed SA-80.

A waiter appeared in front of me with a potbellied pan gun firing hot plastic, his face lambent with disinterest. There was a sad pop like a cheap firework and his eyes turned inward. Instead of giving a single cough and falling, he blotted his copybook by revealing a dynamite vest and exploding into white ash which swirled a little and blew away, some flying into my face and mouth. Murphy the Fed stood on a bit of tilted concrete, her blunt body a silhouette against spilt fire. Smoking in her hand was a little plastic pistol of a simple design that appealed to me. This must have been the girly gun she'd shown Blince. I suspected it had no more weight than its reflection in a mirror. The cylinder looked like a toy Curta calculator. No smarts. Then I noticed the novelty lucite handle containing jelly-eating ants, a practice I believe is cruel and unimaginative.

'You know, Colt is a gateway to other guns.'

'Where's the kid and the oldster?' she asked, walking down the slope with the gun raised. We were having to shout over the mayhem.

'To think I brought that funny dog to your attention - the one that wasn't there when you looked. Now you want to postmark my head with a glint pistol. You lied and I burned my throat swallowing it. But I swallowed it, I did that.'

'Why d'you think I lied?'

'Came on like a religion.'

'How?'

'Told me a little truth while leaving out some of the things I already knew, then added aliens.'

'I didn't lie.'

'You gave me up.'

'No. They found your rail gun. It was under your pillow.'

I had put it under the pillow, that much true.

'Think you'll find them with your showy little cowgirl pistol?'

She thought that over without any obvious embarrassment. 'You denied them,' she concluded.

She glanced around while still trying to cover me. I didn't make a break for it. I wanted to watch her eyes as she tried to work out what she was evading. What true thing couldn't she afford to believe? It was interesting. She advanced on me, the gun still raised. 'Where are they?'

I opened the front passenger door so she would experience the precision vertigo of seeing a gullwing gap in the centre of a blind spot. 'Quick,' I said.

She ducked into the passenger seat and I settled behind the wheel. I took my slimline Armani out the glove box and handed it to the Fed. 'Give me the purse gun.'

She frowned. 'You kidding?'

'I'll tell you when I am.'

She gave me the toon pistol. Leaning out the door, I smashed the butt against the ground until the lucite cracked, and mixed the jelly and ants in with the dirt. I sealed the doors and turned back to the old man and the kid. 'Are you Heber?' I asked the kid. He looked to the old man, turned back to me and nodded, simple. 'And you?' I asked the old man.

'No.'

'What's your name?'

'Ed Novalis.'

'Edna Valis. Never heard the name Edna on a man before.'

I scrutinised him. His sunburned face was delirium stretched over bone. 'Yes, my skull's a barely adequate frame to contain it,' he said, startling the hell out of me. But he was amused. It seemed after too long under the bland sun his brain had turned to varnish. He had one of those long white beards they call a wizard's tail, which he had roped around and around his neck like a scarf.

'When Strobe gets here for cover, we're leaving,' I told them all, and sure enough the security swan swooped in over the battleground, cutting through towers of smoke and releasing a gold polyhedron before peeling away. The holographic claymore unpacked as it fell, each of a hundred fragments expanding into a hundred identical fragments that contained a hundred more unto infinity. Below a certain scale these particles were harmless but even without compression the device created a ricocheting chaos of metal pellets that had everyone pinned down. Everything was coated in dust, dirt and ash the same grey as my Faraday shades as I drove away over breakables and jettisoned ordnance.

I was disappointed to have encountered something as violent and conventional as tonight's exchange. It didn't have the charm of the frenzies of legend, but the resentment that comes from having to pit one's wits against well-armed stupidity persisted. That these short and occasional moments of match and mayhem were a sort of communication - the only form to fully convey certain aspects of the denizens' resentment - I had no doubt. But to deny them their resentment was never seriously considered. In truth the polarising effect of death never helped at all in sorting out a dispute with any finality.

So went my diagnosis at the time. But I wondered then, and wonder now, if part of my lack of enthusiasm was due simply to knowing that this was work already done. Was the uproar acted out every night?

I parked up outside the Reaction and took them inside. 'Toto's an old friend. He's got a sort of hen, out back. It's what he uses for a conscience. It's probably not much good.'

'Well at least they don't bother anyone,' said Murphy.

The bar was empty, only Toto at his post behind the loss counter. He had an all-or-nothing Pound rifle stripped to its threefold form and was reading the obscure scripture on the side of the ammo box. The Pound worked on a principle of motive momentum, taking intention at face value and inducing the physical locality to join in. He looked up, happy.

'There he is,' I hailed. 'What are you so cheerful about, Toto?'

'Oh I just found a raisin, take a look.'

'That's a spider. And this is Toto, everyone. We can only guess at what hatred and revenge smoulders in his heart. Comes peering at the world from the wrong side of an intake fan.'

'You'll be bloated and venting methane before you know it, Atom.'

I asked for the use of his basement and he led us back to a rear door covered in decals with relic irony from a decade ago. Down some steps was a chamber containing a table made of a giant cable spool. The chairs were car seats on bricks. The black walls looked acrylic, the floor plastered in obsolete wolf tickets and cain dollars. The only decoration was a small framed painting of a starling with a tiny machine gun. What I at first took for a pile of coal was actually a heap of huge meaty flies. It wasn't too different from the bar. Murphy looked around the room as if it was beyond help. 'There's antifreeze,' I told them, 'shockers, a bathful of monitor lizards, a flying insect with legs like whiskers, Jade works if you need them. Even a little Gamete, like the best hotels.'

'If these walls could scream,' Toto chuckled. 'This is the very basement where they tied Brute Parker to a chair thinking he was John Stoop impersonating Brute Parker. Those were the town's salad days eh Taff? And locks you could pick with cotton wool.'

We got into some headcrime nostalgia. Whatever happened to Rosa Control? To Findley Taz, born predefeated and honest about it? Gone surely as all those scenes and conversations lost through web decay. It had been a time in which crime and legislative infringement almost simultaneously attained classical heights, the two disciplines operating in lively counterpoint. For a while they had been adding to crime's table of elements at a rate of one a day. Now, without critics wily enough to grasp it, conceptual crime was not processed or appreciated, rotting on the branch. Its special innocence was an obsolete phenomenon. I'd read about some of the final bank heists and the sense of cheerless inhibition those reports conveyed had depressed the hell out of me.

'Betty still working offset?'

'Yeah. Violence longs to be repeated merely - somehow it's never bored.'

'Stand under the light,' I told the kid, and took a good look at him. For miles behind his face there was nothing but blue sky. His energy was smooth as cream. The edges were microscopically frilled and ticklish. I looked away, the marrow in my bones zinging. The kid had the purest vibe I'd ever felt. I stubbed my brain against it, couldn't think about it directly.

Neither the kid nor the old trout said anything, and staring at me seemed to be the only amusement they required. They seemed light-headed at being alive at all.

'Mix everyone a Lively Green,' I told Toto, and showed him a few places where structural alterations to the basement were necessary. He told me rats would soon be using my ribcage as a jungle gym.

'Get out of here!' he shouted, and after making me repeat the instruction carefully back to him, bid me farewell.

As I drove to Betty's Fort I saw my reflection - I was a kind of living scarecrow. I was feeling more acclimatised to the city, its resonances dyeing my mind dark red. Beyond the windshield, the endlessly intricate dance of bastards. Kids pouring acid on the hood of a stranded copcar. A ghost marketeer pushing a warhead in a baby carriage. Hardshell idiots, braying failures and abandoned dogs rotted on the chain. The air was criss-crossed with a density of laws that could strip the skin off a man's head for a moment's inattention. A shriek, a violation, a delectation. Humanity was a species tested so long it should have fallen into baffled despair rather than its present million contradictory positions of utter certainty.

I approached the long Fort under the open muzzle of the moon.

PART TWO

SAMADHI

1

HIGH ROLLER

Betty's Fort was a midtown apartment knock-through with outer walls thicker than blood. Workers had dug up several ranks of ancient terra cotta protesters during the extension and Betty saved a couple for her hallway. She ran this town now, if anyone did. Some say she always had, and since Thermidor was ventilated by Cortez and Cortez was hit by both ends of a truck, she'd become fully evident. In the face of moral teachings many people offset their murders by paying a potential murderer to keep his urges in check, and apparently this was still Betty's main stream of income. The quietest people sometimes rise. Even the infamous mooncow Leon Wardial was circling the world in an armed blimp.

I shot some Jade, left the car and approached this urban keep that had grown while everyone was looking the other way. There was a graded richness across the tarmac that tried to fill me with trance geometries - this was here for the purpose, to waste my time. I'd told her I was coming. I made the sign of the Errorverse, and entered.

Two gunsels braced me for charm in a corridor lined sarcastically with racks of carbines. Then I walked through some notched plastic vegetation and between Chinese door gods into a windowless chamber of blazing black and red decor. Years of accumulated obtainium lined the walls. And between two pyramidal gun drones Betty Criterion sat in a glinting leather armchair black as a beetle, stroking some sort of crustacean that had a knuckleduster for a backbone. She was cartoonish royalty. A face like a saddle bore a mouth unnaturally large like a peony, conflict diamond eyes and ears that wouldn't quit. She was dressed like one of those toys you got as a prize in a claw machine. But despite it all, here was an intelligence that was menacingly still. I felt a mother-of-pearl discomfort.

'There you are, dangling from your head,' she said. 'Been in the wars, I think. Look like a zombie covered in flour.'

'My appearance tells a story. One of panic and failure. The sooner I'm replaced by my corpse-in-waiting the better.'

'Cushioned in loose worms.'

'In a coffin, adjusting to my remains.'

'And for my part, I expect to find my final resting place in a gravel separation plant.'

With courtesies fulfilled, she stood, placed her pet ganglion on her throne and gestured to a kevlar couch. 'Siddown and rest your sense of mystery, Mr Atom.'

I sat. It was nothing I hadn't been subjected to a hundred times. She joined me on the couch. The less pig-like of the guards who had frisked me placed a jetbone tea service on a coffee table built over an antique Hotchkiss Knee cannon, and left quietly. Betty herself poured black pearl tea from a pot with a pearlite grip. On her wrist was an iwatch in the form of a midnight butterfly. 'You're not here to say goodbye, so ask me. Safe conduct?'

'There was an Abrams battle tank at the Gate party tonight. Seems to me you're the only non-brotherhood who can rustle up a tank these days.'

'So?'

'So what's with the Heber kid? He looks blank to me, but everyone's up on their hind legs. What do you know about him?'

'I've never heard of Heber Partenheimer.'

'I didn't tell you his second name.'

'How careless of me. I have given something away.' She didn't look at all upset. 'But identity's a strange one. The necessity for extraneous measures has been forced upon us by law, Mr Atom. To operate in this acquisitive world we require many IDs, or none - whatever is needed to avoid being owned. Do you know that it was once common for people to use the name of their pets as a decoy? There was an entire generation of hounds who went about with full and human-sounding names. Frank Murkowski. Richard B. Myers. Senorita Clemencia Arango. There is even a Professor Traven who lives in the Terminal suburbs, who named his pet Heber Partenheimer.'

I sipped the sweet tea and gazed at her antique

jukeboxes and a couple of those automated ammo dispensers they used to have in malls. Two boosted paintings hung on opposite walls. Here was Ernst's *Numb Town*, its alien architecture of massive pillars slathered in spinach and bat anatomy. And there was Frances Castle's *Cowgirl*, a bullseye of a red inflatable sheriff about to duel sans gun or clothing, covertly crossing her fingers.

'You enabled the retirement of two of my Mexicans,' Betty stated mildly.

'They were yours?'

That was awkward. I was going to die here obviously.

'Nice work,' she said. 'They were about to betray me. Junco has.'

'The Thistle. He's good, actually. Pulled a blocker on a truck, point-blank. Never seen anything like it.'

'Hmm. Well, he's Pivot's man now. I may have to arrange to have him shot a little.'

'Pivot wants the kid?'

'Not exactly. For reasons of his own he wants him to run free.'

'And Chief Blince?'

'One should not expect a coherent ideology from a pullulating blob of junk DNA.' Betty repeated the general opinion that Blince was so like a massive amoeba he could reproduce by binary fission. 'And is therefore a surprisingly self-sufficient man,' she added. 'And his implied claim to at least one of the attributes of god was endorsed the first time he punished an innocent man.'

'I heard he's named his jowls Terry and Christopher.'

'That is true,' she said solemnly.

'What's this religion Parker's fallen for?'

'A goddess with a thousand arms, a gun in every one. He has suffered the failure of purpose all men are heir to.'

'And you?'

'I believe there's no act so terrible that god won't forgive it if it has time in its busy schedule. And nothing it hasn't done itself, obviously.'

'That why you can't wait to finish one murder before starting the next one?'

'I haven't murdered in years,' she said in mock outrage. 'Not since Cortez, actually.'

'A murder so sweet it had a rose named after it.'

'Yes, it was recorded for training purposes. He couldn't really handle heading the mob, that man. Spent the average evening snorting his Ma's ashes off his own bicep. In fact his stance of avoidance had provided his right arm so much exercise in repeatedly covering his eyes that it had grown outsize and beefy, the bicep thick as a steering column. I ran him over with a monster truck and he offered no resistance. In his defence, he hasn't died one iota since. But they made to take the accomplishment from me by declaring it a crime and, all being innocent until proven guilty, I was "free to leave". I'm still here, naturally. Murders should be acts of definition, not of criticism.'

It was all very civilised. I couldn't tell if the Jade was throttling or dialling up - maybe the latter. She was a big glass of smarts.

'People still try to avoid understanding how I got here, but corrosion is detailed, not vague. Born into bad times, graffiti on the incubator, umbilical tied with accident tape. Did you know I worked in the water cannery, swimming through the most mundane of public reflexes? Bullets have all the qualities of hysteria, Mr Atom - they're fast, go where they're pointed, and travel in herds. But then I thought, well, people do fire bullets, and other people receive them, so who am I to stand in the way? Flying bullets were just like please and thankyou in such circles, even then. Say the right thing and they'd fire ten, eleven of them - as many as you like. All close together like demands for cash. And no foreign travel. I saw it could make more money than war. Knowing that "Money can't buy happiness" is said either honestly by the stupid or falsely by the smart. Murder, in old currency. I merely committed the crime, I don't claim to have originated it.'

She was looking me in the face as if peering around a corner - trying to see something.

'After a while you get to know things, Mr Atom. The different shades of red according to the wound location. That winging someone is like an affair - they get to thinking it's more serious than you do. And like a marriage, a murder happens on a burst of enthusiasm - the regret comes later. A fired bullet operates in one direction, like destruction. Lower killing upper class is unnatural murder, upper killing lower is execution or excusable error.'

I was point-blank in her precious stone stare.

'You trying to corrupt my morals?' I said with a little irony.

'I can't corrupt or install what you don't have. What you call your virtue is someone else's. You just shrugged it on like a coat.'

'No. You're not seeing me clearly enough.'

There were a thousand folds in the air between us where meaning could get caught and flipped around. Was the tea drugged?

I coughed.

'You don't go with the favour system?'

'As far back as I can recall I was frightened of favours,' she said. 'To owe something, to be owed, it's terrible. I mix my personality with yours and we get a third one I'm not in control of. Too messy. I never had the sort of complacency required to put myself unreservedly at the disposal of the law. You shouldn't mind - you who seem to give off rays of inconvenience. You know, I respect that.'

The space in here was untranslatable. No visitor could go off and reproduce the specific emphases. She'd probably installed a contradiction in the room that slipped observers down a precise evasion vector like a trapdoor and chute. I mentally repeated the local zenbit for clearing the mind, 'Anything a potato is wrong about...'

'Your approval is an imposition.'

'You're right,' she nodded. 'I apologise.'

I put down the teacup and stood, going over to look at a teak cabinet displaying a set of Turkish plague knives and an ordeal mask with inner blades. The pause allowed me to circumnavigate her arguments and look back at my own - the entire vista left a lot to be desired. I was some sort of clog-wearing hen. Again I wondered what the hell I was doing here.

'I'm a winter wasp already,' I said, peering at some glass coins. 'I should be out of Beerlight. This place is dying, I've warned about it before.'

Betty laughed. 'I've been pegging away at the task of bleeding it dry for years now, and the street's still full of bastards and ballistic neurasthenics.'

'Amid denial things seem to run out slowly, so when things finally run out altogether, well - it'll seem kinda sudden. I probably shouldn't have come back.'

'Why'd you leave in the first place?'

'Got tired of forever waking up with bits of puzzle stuck to my face. That and the sheer boredom of warehouse standoffs.'

'And where have you been?'

'Maybe I've been living as a penniless sponge-diver. I'm only flesh and blood, as far as you know.'

'Ofcourse. I appreciate you telling me yourself.'

Above the black marble fireplace hung crossed foils. 'You can fence?'

'I learnt when I was angry.'

'You're not like the old mob. Don't so obviously throw your weight around.'

'Remind you of anything?' she asked, pouring more tea. 'Neither of us are so involved, Mr Atom. I stay above it by seeming to run it. You stay aside from it by being ... what was it they said about you? You're *not all there.*'

I'd started studying the hardcopy bookshelves that stood between the recessed lighting. Eddie Gamete ran through them like a rash. 'You're a Gamete fan.'

'I thought it was a real philosophy until I tried to holster my gun in it. I think his insights were dangerous to no-one and quite forgettable among the people it would attack. Why expose an edifice that's already been reduced to its reinforcement rods?'

'So why keep these?'

'Sentiment. I like that he was a variable value that threw everything off its centre for a moment. Dead for five years. Not always an easy time for an artist. What about you?'

'I think it's sad that he's hotel-standard now. That kind of acceptance inoculates people against his effects. It brings tears to the surface of my head.'

I thought of people's strange reactions to the oldster who'd long since shucked his shell after apparently flouncing off in a sort of creative tantrum. He flourished ideas from air that people preferred to remain empty. His relentless lack of duplication went far beyond the perverse. Many felt a mental revulsion, the perilous essence of the original as radioactively terrifying as an angel.

'You've got *The World Cup Ordination of Schott-ner Kier.*'

'Yes. Borrow it if you like.'

'I've never seen it. It's totally rare.'

'It's yours. Now sit down. I'd like to read your future in the cards.'

She opened a Russian malachite jewellery box and removed a block of gypsy fortune-telling cards. As I returned to the couch she was laying the square cards on the coffee table - they were black lacquer-painted with a load of Palekh-style symbols I didn't understand.

'Luck - it grants and dispossesses, aids and forsakes. This it does with formidable precision and force, yet - many would insist - without emotion or malice. What do you think of the idea?'

'It's very nice, what I can see of it.'

'Don't you believe?'

'I suppose everyone grieves in a different way.'

'That sort of fixed-blade logic'll tear up your pants. Bad luck is the shadow of a thing too cowardly to show itself from head to tail. Isn't it interesting that government will operate in the same way? Its crime is concealed from end to end by the "common good". Now, let's see what we have here. *Stars:* blindness to what is before you. Distraction will force you to make a series of mistakes. *Anchor:* you have put down your anchor in the wrong place, a mistake difficult to correct. *Book:* a secret disclosed to you will become public knowledge. This should not concern you if you have conducted your affairs honestly. *Fire:* fire will envelop your heart." It looks bad for you, Mr Atom.'

I suppose I disliked it. 'Seems kinda nebulous. Everything needs a context, after all.'

'"Everything" is the one thing that doesn't.'

I stared at her.

She seemed amused. 'Well, it's after all no business of mine.'

'I guess I better fill my pockets with excuses and jump in the river,' I said, standing to go. I remembered to take the book.

'Atom,' she called out. I turned at the door. She was standing by one of the ammo dispensers. 'I know you've got tiny dynamind. For a shamus you seem particularly clueless. Don't throw out the baby to spite your own face.'

It was daylight when I emerged from that strange meeting. I capped it feeling I even liked her a little.

It surprised me. I'd heard she was just a fat bitch.

I felt drunk, seeing symbols in the sky, plus a few clouds that were apparently no longer in use. And I knew someone was following me - pointlessly, as it turned out.

2

HAMMER INTO ANVIL

'Engage windshield display.'

Heading back to the Reaction, I checked the gap and dredge. There was no mention of Heber Partenheimer. Or Edna Valis. In Beerlight innocence is a worthless commodity. Since meeting the kid I'd been assuming he was a decoy and that it was all about the old man, but there was nothing. I took a look at Parker and his gun god, and a closer look at Pivot. He was ultrajincho, and longterm in the law racket. While mayors were propelled upward by a hybrid of chance and stupefying pliancy, DAs ascended by an insular revelling in expedience and personal enrichment and there a legal ritual where it had to appear that a really first-rate thing had been allowed. Generally neither lasted longer than a radish, but Pivot had been up for months. I did not understand what had happened to make the difference. My little reverse engine was scrambling over unlabelled groupings and incoherent hierarchies. I scratched around for Betty's lead. Professor Traven turned out to be the scientist author of a psychological study *Beyond Indignation* and was living in a Terminal suburb called Longreen. We'd be fine if we avoided the madmaxers.

When I got to the Delayed Reaction I entered the building by the back door and descended to the basement to find the kid and the old man playing cards amid strange cargo. The kid looked up in honest and open wonder, his face pale as an aspirin and his blonde hair curly like an ice cream. He had a Jade needle hanging from the middle of his forehead and Old Man Valis had five crowded round his nose like a starnose badger. 'This basement isn't for the faint-hearted, Mr Atom,' said the oldster, and pointed to Murphy. 'That one's been on some mad crusade to get us talking. Boy, she hit me upside the head eleven times before I even guessed what she wanted.'

Murphy stubbed her cigarette on the wall with a fierce gesture. Her hair was jagged. She was burnt around the edges. 'You left me here like a prisoner, Atom. With that Toto creature as a guard. I could spit.'

'Don't - you can't afford to lose any weight.'

'She's a live one alright,' chuckled the old man. 'Plaguing me with questions. Guess we know who wears the pants in this barn!'

'Did you attack these two?'

'Honestly I had no sense of punching them very hard.'

I was bored. Believing she could have no idea

why, I explained it in finely-crafted detail, after which I was astonished to see her anger increase.

The kid and the old man exchanged cards like the common cold.

'Gather all you've decided to make yours, take the back way out and gather in the alley, with some clothes on.'

I went back upstairs and approached the saloon bar. Someone was talking to Toto. I cracked the door a little and peered in. One of Betty's men had him covered with a La France automatic rifle. The piglike gunsel had a flat nose and wide flesh-tunnelled piercings so his earlobes resembled trigger guards.

Toto stood there evading, obfuscating, sneering, shouting and doing whatever else entered his mind. He didn't turn into a quivering balloon animal - I would have been surprised if he had. But he did a good job of spreading his arms to indicate the liquor bottles behind him. 'All this can be yours.'

'Are you calling me fat, you bastard? You're the fat bastard.'

Toto struck what he probably thought was a chastened pose but succeeded only in looking like an ape.

'Where's Atom? Where's the kid?'

In answer to his enquiry Toto gave a gesture of dismissal into which he managed to invest a wholly inappropriate quality of saintliness, enraging the gunsel instantly. 'Doing me a hard favour are you?' the pigman asked, 'by deigning to ignore me? You imperious -'

Toto produced the Pound gun, firing and ducking instantly behind the bar. The gun's pulse grid mapped the room and propelled every local unfixed object after the bullet. Bottles, glasses, knives, guns, chairs and beernuts stormed at the gunsel in a deafening thunderclap of blood and splinters. Before he hit the floor I had slammed the door and run out back.

I piled the old man, the kid and the girl into the Mantarosa. Edna was cheerful, the bone-haired loon. 'Curiosity is honest or it is inoperative,' he crooned. It was a Gamete cliche - apparently there were fans even in the Fadlands. That reminded me, and I flung the Gamete book at the back seat before peeling out.

Through the Portis Thruway and out of Beerlight into the fringes of Our Fair State. Fewer street skulls and more voodoo masts as we approached the Terminal state line. Next to me Murphy put her bare feet up on the dash and injected the inside of her thigh, tarpaper shacks and derelict emplacements blurring by behind her. We were crossing through intermediate jurisdictions of lopsided shelters, dry irrigation canals and telegraph poles stumped for fuel or barricades. The road fed into the hood like accelerated information. In the back seat the kid and the old man fixed some Jade, for which they seemed to have got a taste, and the kid was looking at *Schottner Kier*. It occurred to me that, by a number of astounding twists of fate, he had at some point learned to read. Where? Compared to the Fadlands and its hollowphernalia, even this burning distance of waste was a fertile paradise.

Murphy had apparently sauntered all over these two in the basement. If they knew something considered of value, the smart play was to ditch them in this bayonet wasteland. But the kid looked guileless, the greenest kid since Leon Wardial whose reference to a 'plural-barreled shotgun' had provoked near-lethal scorn.

Peroxide clouds in a sky the colour of stone-washed jeans. We rolled through marooned neighborhoods sentried by creosote plants. Lux Murphy's canary-yellow hair flickered in desert wind. We were shot at only once. 'Got my good side?' Murphy yelled at the hidden sniper. Then we hit an atoll of part-inhabited houses, a surprise district of shattered answering machines and little black gardens. The suburbs: every car looks satisfied. Dust-covered trees like antique furniture, open tanks of iron-grey water and the churn of generators. Here and there I saw gun barrels and silencers, hidden in plain view as wind chimes. Some of the windows had glass.

We parked up outside number 12 and walked across a little square yard of dead devil grass to the bleached and crumbling facade of Traven's house. The doorknocker was a ring in the mouth of a German. 'Let me do the braying,' I whispered, and knocked. No reply. We stalked cautiously around back, past a mushroom hut made from the buried shell of a VW microbus. A glassless conservatory was fronted by decking, design of the damned. Skirting it, we found a rear door. 'Anyone home?'

The middle-aged man who appeared at the door had estranged hair, potato-coloured clothes and legs that met several times before reaching his waist. His right arm was made of white plastic and with his left he aimed at me a summer savings semi-automatic. 'What name are you using?' he demanded, and waved the gun at the others. 'And you.' Then he stopped, seeing the kid, and lowered the weapon.

'I'm called Atom,' I said. 'Do you use the name B. Traven?'

'I don't know anything,' he said, still staring dazedly at the kid.

'Be more specific.'

He considered a moment. 'For that you'll have to come in. But leave *that*,' and he pointed at the kid, 'outside if you don't mind.'

The old man elected to stay in the yard with Heber. Traven frowned at Edna as me and Murphy entered, then seemed to dismiss whatever was bothering him and closed the door.

It was a dim room of tattooed curtains and un-dead armchairs. Stubborn old moments in frames intervened in the walls. There was a dead fakewood TV with a tweed jacket over its shoulders. The only sound was a single daytime cicada and a copper orrery in the form of an ammonite that ticked away the weight of ages. Murphy and I placed aside old copies of *Tentative* magazine and sat in a couple of chairs that seemed to have been sewn out of dust.

'I don't get many visitors except a few book exorcists and the occasional dismal raiding party,' Traven said. He had an Irish accent and a nervous energy about him. He put the Daewoo on a coffee table and did not sit down. 'You know there's alot of gas bandits belting around the local desert in feral cars with Jesus piranhas on their fenders. Who sent you?'

'Nobody sends me anywhere.'

'Not if you're aware of it anyway. Who's the girl?'

'Murphy. Coke train.'

'I haven't had great experiences with Feds,' he said, gesturing to his right arm.

'I'm a free agent now,' said Murphy.

'Your course of exhaustion was science, is that right?' I asked him.

'If you're here about the kid out there, you know that already. I could relate the story wittily, emotionally, even accurately if need be.'

'We'll take the accurate version.'

'As you wish. But don't tell this to a living soul.'

'Can I tell Download Jones?'

'Is he alive?'

'No.'

'That's fine. I worked at the Armstrong Death Labs at Brooks Air Force Base in Texas. Top-secret crypto clearance. Psychological warfare and chemical grudgecraft. Slapping folk with campaign pins doped with sodium fluoride. Crazy savages ate that election. One day I thought I'd leapfrog an anxious meeting. I was reading *Bleak House* and burst out laughing as everyone does when that fella spontaneously combusts for no reason.'

'Oh, I know what you mean. It's like that thing at the end of Forster's vampire novel *Howards End.*'

The Fed girl brightened, surprising me. 'When that guy gets flattened by the wardrobe?'

'And nobody cares, that's right!' Traven said. 'A comic masterstroke at the end of a dreary ordeal.'

'I wonder if he planned towards it,' I said, 'or just gave up and threw caution to the wind, exploding with laughter at his own mischief?'

'I don't know. But in any case, the Dickens

thing got me thinking. We're all just bags of chemicals basically, and a bomb operates when a barrier between two chemicals is removed. Since the delineation between civilians and combatants became meaningless - a drift led by our own armies abroad - we'd been exploring ways to give everyone a combat role, to win the masses to their destruction. A conjuror's dependence on the credulous doesn't have a military behind it, but I did. Apart from the towering number of moral objections, why not flood the limbic-diencephalic system with nitrophagal propellants - this becomes the primary neurotransmitter at the reasoning centres of the brain. The bomb is primed. It also aids the transmission of ideas and optimises the conditions for detonation.'

'Sounds slow.'

'You *bet* it was trash. I wanted something as immediate as an impact bomb, which relies on resistance. The very fact that a building wishes to remain standing is kinetic justification for it to fall upon impact. It's the resistance principle. Extended to people, it allows us to claim that those who resist violence are provoking a violent response. Those who resist being killed will likely end up dead - isn't it often so? I removed a sample of fissionary diatoms from a four-foot-long rootmouth jellyfish with a view to placing a little metanovic filament in that grey nothing-spider which is the calyx of the brain. Everyone said "You can't do that." Ofcourse when people claim something is impossible they usually mean they believe you *shouldn't* do it, and sure enough when I tried I found it was perfectly possible, even easy. The theory was that when our chemical met one of the more mundane chemicals in the brain - norepinephrine, for instance - it would start off a biochemical chain reaction that led quickly to a detonation. You could x-ray the head and not detect a thing. The only problem was the trigger, the means of breaking the separating barrier. We worked on it for years, staying awake so as to miss nothing. We had hamster cages bedded with shredded Canadian holocaust documents and the most sarcastic computer since Flowers built the first. Orgies figured minimally during the research. In fact we didn't have any. It was one of those phases when the government experienced such a surfeit of misery they had to ship a lot of it to the Middle East, and the pressure was on. What breaks through mental barriers? Originality, ofcourse. Was this an unfortunate answer? Not really. It was something prohibited and deplored to the point that an accidental trigger was pretty unlikely. But you never know...'

A tired dog wandered in and collapsed, perhaps dead. What I'd thought was a cicada was a little geigercounter it wore on its collar.

'Why install it so young?'

'Kids are very conformist, I mean to peer pressure, the crowd. They're taught ideopathic history - no known cause. At best they can have a philosophy made from found objects. It was felt that in a child the slightest hint of the original would set it off. But that one, we weren't sure what was going wrong with it. He was an orphan, and now seemed as good a time as any to make him into a walking advertisement for devastation. Partenheimer's head or "stupidity turret" seemed perfect for our purposes. We tested him at a field station in an abandoned missile silo. He was behind a blast-proofed screen and we piped in a series of ideas and images, waiting for the one that would tip him over, a fertile singularity. We termed it "rich zero". At first he was too toddly and bright to be observed with any accuracy. But he began to show evidence of saintliness, even boredom. Meanwhile our computer models suggested that the detonation would be massive, unmanageable.'

'Did you ever work it out?'

The Professor sat down. 'Theories. Mine was that he was compartmentalising - storing any originality away in a mental vault. If that was so, god help us if it burst its hinges.'

I thought about the kid, his face filled with a calm, quietly radiant disinclination.

'Was he always like this?' Murphy asked. 'Kinda simple-minded?'

'I could never really tell. He was quiet.'

'Is it possible he stays this way as a defence mechanism, to prevent his realising anything?'

'I don't know. Yes, perhaps. To evade is a bedrock instruction humanity must follow, even when all else has been discarded. In his case it would be a means of self-preservation. In any case the government contractors ordered Heber to be disposed of. I wasn't happy with it, and also knew if he died the separation barrier would dissolve, resulting in ignition. I had taken on the protective colouration of hypocrisy, more in sorrow than in anger.'

I watched Traven, the rods and cones of his morality pointing in different directions. In an earlier age he would have been an honest man, maybe.

'Imagine my annoyance at being saddled with such a serious matter. Yes I was in a tight corner, a very tight corner indeed.'

'Have you heard of open corners? Looks like a corner but it actually flutes open into a sort of exit.'

'Hell of a thing, it was,' said Traven as though he hadn't heard. 'I had to keep him alive with a margin of safety. But even today it's possible to blunder into an idea now and again. Then I hit on it.'

'The Fadlands,' I said.

All at once he surged to his feet, taking me by surprise. 'It was perfect! Under a rigor mortis sky lay an entire chunk of landmass so lacking in real mental sustenance it had surpassed blandness and gone into reverse, denuded of refusal or exam-ination, sap or invention! Nothingness repeated across the flavourless drifts of a trend desert! Epidemic technology and lack of independent imagination keep things fast and hollow. It's really only a rather terminal version of the general way we avoid saying anything interesting because we know it upsets people. But Heber would be completely safe among flocking re-run heads. So I abducted him and set him loose in the vacuum.

'The project went belly-up, obviously. The team was disbanded. There was even an internal enquiry at which the board were carefully shocked in chorus. I told them exactly what I'd done and they had no trouble believing me. I consulted a law book, the contents of which I found to resemble the ravings of a lone crackpot. Do you understand that when a collective identity is formed it has a very distinctive intelligence of its own, always lower than the average among its individuals? My guilt was cushioned by the condemnation of others and the bonanza of justification that provoked. I was ordered to confine my attention to areas of research that had already been exhausted. For millennia humanity's been learning with the handbrake on, after all - that was the argument. But a stopped clock never boils, Mr Atom. No matter how unpopular and sensible it may appear, science has created the misery and systems of drainage that separate us from the barbarians. Humanity is capable of amazing, even useless things, and many people worship science from the same general tiredness as others attend church.'

'Church?' asked Murphy.

'Ancestral buildings purporting to act as a dimensional propellant,' I explained.

'I quit, Mr Atom. And for a while nobody seemed to care. But when an explosion levelled the Pentagon, maps got a terrific shock. And the militia decided the Medulla Obliterata was an idea parted too young from its mother. What will evil not do, when circumstances make extraordinary demands of it? I found myself on a high security prison island, in a cell so quiet I could hear myself bleeding. A mental breakdown landed on me like a shrieking chimp. My madness has been reconsecrated five times since then, as every year the performance is repeated by one party or another. I tell them I left the apocalypse in my other coat.'

'We've noticed the various interested parties.

Even Chief Blince.'

'Oh, that one. He's essentially a giant gauge boson for the force of ignorant action, with a spin value of one. I argued he had nothing on me because it was impossible to prove a negative. You can imagine how well that was received.' As he cradled his false arm, his face bore a series of taboo expressions, ending in grief.

'Interrogations aren't all bad. Sometimes it's nice to have someone else take charge and tell you what to do.'

'Indeed. The electrode has become my most particular friend. Meeting with your life takes years, an accidental meeting - it won't let you get away soon unless you're firm with it. As a scientist I wanted to emerge nuclear from something horribly grand. Certainly I expected rather more than a walk-on part in my own life. But I never regretted the decision to free that exploited child. It was a crowning experience for me. In that act I defined myself' - he spread his arms - 'and became the chubby pariah you see before you.'

'You're not chubby.'

'So they've taken even that from me.' His arms flapped to his sides and he hung his head. 'I've been here since the Time of Dead Birds, getting mopey and meaningful. All I do now is dick around. I've worked as a pin chimp at the bowling alley, then taking aerial photos of people's cats by just standing over them and taking a picture, then making wigs for ghosts, and some of those interim professions that sprung up briefly - I was a printbleacher for a while, and a battery man until the scavenging went dry. Have you heard of the Turing test, Mr Atom -

to determine if someone is a real human being?'

'No, I haven't.'

'If they try and convict you for no crime, chemically castrate you and drive you to suicide despite your being instrumental in winning their war, they're human.'

'What's your advice on the kid?'

'Don't say or do anything interesting, don't let him read, and for god's sake keep him off Jade.'

In the silence that followed I noticed old man Edna was stood in the doorway. He looked as disconcerted as a pig on a Ferris wheel.

3

NOT WAVING BUT COOKING

Traven made us some sort of stone stew out of
nettles, mushrooms and cigarettes. There was also
tea made apparently from eyeshadow. To me he
supplied bandages. My hand wound zinged like
sweetened lightning. We were invited to stay the
night. An obscure room held alot of apparatus
but didn't look to have been used in a long while.
Traven rummaged through the equipment. 'I've
been cataloguing meaningless changes on the
inner surface of this funnel, do you see? I have less
and less conviction that the exercise is worth it.'

'It's not, obviously.'

'You're right. I'm all washed up.'

In an open barn what we'd thought was the fore
of a train was a dead turbine. We looked it over for
kit, found nothing usable.

This house of used retorts was tragic. When
darkness fell I headed out to the car. The street

night was a black magnet dragging downwards. Trees hissed like dissolving codeine and dim tumbleweeds blew by in a creepy way. The kid was sat on the kerb, his head bent over *Schottner Kier*. Maybe it was like I told Betty, books only inoculate against ideas' real effect. We all compartmentalise so as not to have to freak out. 'How's the book?'

The kid looked up, eyes like a cartoon.

I left him to it. I got in the car, locked it, pulled the scale gear and clambered into the back as the stepdown initiated. The back seat of Planckward planks elongated into a staircase etherically canted to form a slant entry into sidespace. I let go and quickly hit a chicane, a fold where reality had been dodged. The world was full of them now, billions to any geographical instant, and the trained sense could feel them out like the ridges in a lenticular print. I teased the crack a little wider and went through, hidden by locating myself amid the matter the world hid from itself. The concomitant drench of truth was both refreshing and ugly, blazing and muted, a very particular quality of bright sourness. I flew through discarded fact, strong and strongly denied; over history, its blurring ranks of petrified reprisal speeding into concurrent strips. You know something is not physical when it has no temperature. The shadow of a flower doesn't hold its colour.

Then the almost unbearable temporal thickening as I valved into the small anteroom we called 'the concourse'. After a few minutes curled up like a fist, I stood unsteadily and pushed the door into Madison's safe house, far from morality's equator. It was designed like a hotel at the bottom of the sea, all blue domed ceilings, thermal mass walls, pillars of poured white glass, arched doors and round windows that brought in the sun. Beyond the frontage of one-way camouflage glass and past the gleaming white-sand beach was the gently rippled amethyst of the ocean. Why be awed by the immensity of obstacles and not by the immensity of nature? Sometimes we cannot fully respond to a new dimension - the less adjacent ones can feel incongruent and may vibrate quite a bit even when idling. But I've found the present works better in territories that don't mirror the rest of the world.

'Maddy?'

'Taff? I'm in the bath.'

I went in, took off my burnt rags and got in opposite her.

'What the hell happened to your hair?'

I ruffled my own scalp happily. 'You like it? It caught on fire.'

'And third-degree burns, missing fingers, flesh-wounds. Are you in pain?'

'Don't get me started. They're all hepped up on ritual and mutual surveillance over there.'

We looked at each other between her legs. It was like driving down the Golden Gate Bridge. Her breasts loved each other.

'How is it?' she asked.

'It's their last chance not to do anything right and they're taking full advantage. Some are claiming civilisation is on the mend asymmetrically. There are still millions of contrahuman, contranatural and contradictory laws sloshing around, and barely enough healthy land into which to push a pin. Nobody really knows what day of the week it is and there hasn't been a decent burial anywhere in years.'

'How's the tech?'

I told her about the hardscrabble cannibalism and systematic avoidance at large. Most potential tech had died by humanity's shortfall, as people found themselves less and less concerned with artificial longevity and neural interfacing, and more concerned with finding something - anything - to eat.

'But there's an exception. Remember when guns got smart? Fire-by-wire. Only enhancements really, we still directed them. But by introducing the etheric pulse grid and a set of criteria we gave them philosophy and they really flowered.'

'The Lotus Gun.'

'The first really sentient one supposedly, yeah. And people thought the issue of gun rights had come too late because most guns still piggy-backed humanity and humanity was finished. But there's been some sort of leap way beyond the days of non-aspirational firearms. Apparently this Calvarius construct has developed way beyond single precept guns. It's worshipped, even by Parker.'

'The man who holds god's bullet in his mouth.'

'Who'd always been vanilla, mainly.'

Maddy was smiling lazily. I wanted to eat the top of her head like a chocolate egg; live in the palm of her hand; dive into her blue swimming pool heart. 'Ah, Maddy. I met you in a sniper's nest and you never let up.'

'I should think not, you dumb goose.'

'That reminds me, Strobe's gone AWOL. His signal's disappeared.'

'Probably off breaking someone's arm with his wing. We all need some downtime. I don't understand why you're still using the Atom personality.'

'It still blends a little. They're cocooned in noir over there, even now. Though they seem to get more elaborately curt every day. I still haven't completely aligned to the indigenous fanatical traditions. I'm not that smart Maddy but surrounded by them it's like running in one-quarter gravity. I've taken so much Jade my head feels like a medicine ball.'

'You're talking as if you're going back.'

'I am.'

After a silence, Maddy stood up and stepped out of the bath. I'd need a siege ladder to reach her ass. Towelling off, she resumed in tirade mode. 'I gave you permission for your final fling or whatever it is. To get it out of your system and get back.'

'Permission?'

She stared candidly at me.

'Okay, permission. But I'm completely gay for you Maddy, you know that.'

'Come on Taff, we so busted our asses getting this place set up during the slow apocalypse and all. We're safe here. History doesn't have the momentum to climb our stairs.'

When we'd left Beerlight way back, the President of China had just broken up the Great Wall so that when viewed from space it said I'M WITH STUPID and pointed across the Pacific. America was no longer viewed as a forgivable adolescent but as an embarrassingly challenged adult.

'You've already done sansara, baby. Stick a fork in their ass and turn them over. Forgive them and don't let them stand in your way.'

'That's what I'm going to do now.'

'It'll be like one of those nightmares, Taff - where you can't find your way back to the beer garden.'

'I feel like I got unfinished business there. Closure.'

'Closure already happened. There's only *other* people's business in Beerlight.'

'I'm not in Beerlight, I'm in the Terminal burbs. Deep masks and chainlink families. It's becoming Fadland, with everything else.'

'Is Beerlight a hold-out?'

'Only just. It's thin. Right now I could fashion a better city out of snot.'

She pulled on her pants. 'Is it suicide by cop, Taff, like Jesus?'

'I'm coming back. It's a final fling, like you said.'

'Morbid curiosity's what it is. It can't be pretty.'

'I saw a nice bird over there, a white one.'

'A dove?'

'It was made of pipe cleaners and had a beer cap for an eye. In the Delayed Reaction Bar. But it was pretty.'

'The Reaction, that old place?'

She put a watch on each wrist, set to two different times.

'Toto was right, bars burn last. I need a gun. Can't find the Glory.'

'I'm not your armourer anymore, Taff.'

She walked out. I got out of the bath and followed her into the workshop. 'Toolmaker then.'

'Inventor. Researcher. You're dragging us backward into the ball pit with those children.'

'What do you know about cortexial payloads?'

She sighed. 'Fissionaries. A myth, basically. The holy grail of the MK-Ultra crowd for a while - Medulla Ballistica. But it's an urban legend as far as I know.'

I thought about that a while. 'I need a sidearm and a sidespace holster.'

'I can make a pouch but subcached ordnance won't make it through the valve. It'll fuse inside you.'

She was looking through tools, and turfed out a blowtorch.

'Just the joeypouch then.'

'Ask Parker's gun god where the Glory's gone. From what you've been saying it's probably taken the opportunity to evolve. Now put your left hand on the worktop and count to three.'

'One.'

I woke in the bedroom staring at the jungle-painted ceiling and hearing the waves. I held my left hand in front of my face. It was black and pink and sealed over.

Maddy walked in. The gravity used from the soles of her feet to the top of her head was a holy sacrament, in my opinion. But still I began evasive manoeuvres. Why?

'So,' I said, 'I started to blather about them who settle for the golden mean between propaganda and actuality, clueless and painless. You're right, it's deader than charcoal. So I'll ride a coffin as it's lowered into the grave, whooping like a cowboy.'

'How much Jade are you on Taff?'

'I dreamt you'd come and make my excuses for me.'

'I asked a question. What are you on?'

'Today?'

I thought about it.

'Jade, Edenblood. Er, Piracetam. Jade. Inverse agonized Suritozole. Rolipram. Soup made of cigarettes and a Jade chaser. Then a little Jade. And I took some Jade.'

'You said Jade before. How much are you taking?'

'Mushrooms?'

'Jade.'

As with a billion other matters, I didn't have a clue. Flying shrapnel had allowed me scant opportunity to think about it or anything. 'It's not that easy.'

'It's not that hard.'

'Time for me to go,' I told her, sitting up. I found and pulled on some unburned clothes. At a sudden thought, I felt around the area of my appendix, where my hand slipped ghostly inside me as if into empty air. 'Thanks.'

'And meanwhile I'll just be looking good by the window.'

I kissed her, and started toward the door.

'A pipe-cleaner bird, Taff? Really?'

I turned and looked at her. I didn't know what to say.

'They're done, Taff. It's all just about done.'

'I have to see it through,' I told her. I looked at my left half-hand and held it up. 'Thanks for mending me, baby.'

I returned to the anteroom, approaching the far wall and its window to nowhere like the collar of a well. I emerged from the etheric crawlspace into the Mantarosa, parked in the suburban night.

Everyone was asleep but Traven. I found him in the smashed conservatory, smoking a nylon cigarette. Desperation was stretched over his life like skullskin. Broken glass crunched under my boots. 'You disturb my ongoing adaptation to defeat,' he said. 'They said it would pass. But ofcourse it doesn't, as you probably know. People forgive themselves too readily.'

'You can't run while you're kicking yourself.'

Forgotten people get complicated in different ways. Some become compassionate and amoral. Others evince the vegetable rectitude of statues. Traven's soul seemed clearcut by exhaustion. He had cooled off enough to reflect upon his circumstances but this had not readied him for the sudden reality of the kid's return.

'Who's the old man?'

'Edna. He's been out in the wilderness living off Skittles and wild honey. Takes care of little Johnny Warhead.'

Traven frowned. Then he resumed smoking.

'We're heading back to Beerlight tomorrow,' I told him.

'Maybe he'll be as safe amid that mummified mobsterism as in the Fadlands. I was interested to see the shard of apparently non-predatory propulsion you're using for a car. How's it work?'

'It's basically a rolling evasion amplifier. Operates by deceiving the road, refusing to admit to a geographical position. If you're precise in your aversions you're precise in your navigation.'

'Yes, though at the beck of every circumstance.'

'Unlimited context obliterates any argument.

The dimensions are all of a flowing piece, but we partition it up, number these partitions and limit ourselves to three or four.'

'I know. But I'm increasingly convinced that this space-time axis is entirely ornamental. What happens here is not meant to be taken seriously. My life has been a daily halloween of patience and postponement. Academia's attempts to prove otherwise have wasted their time and yours.'

'You put it much better than I could,' I said in appeasement.

Traven raised his eyebrows. 'That's big of you.'

I left him in the lonely lighthouse of his head. It was only later that I felt the respect due him. He had *seen* the car.

4

THE BATTLE OF SOKO INTERSTATE

Morning light went about switching on parts of the room. I went out to find the others gathering at the parking gap. The Fed was acting shifty. Here's where I noticed her nose at last. It was nothing special.

A halo outlined Heber's moving figure like a victim chalkline. This celestial conduct unnerved one and all, but Edna still smiled at everything. 'As the rhyme goes: "We're all still here, no-one has gone away."' He got into the back of the car, then poked his head out. '"Acting much too well and procrastinating."' Then he added, more quietly, 'We eat hours and vomit hours,' and dodged his head back in again. The last part was Gamete. The kid got in beside him as Professor Traven emerged from the house, his failures trailing behind him like a dead parachute.

'I want to give you something,' Traven said, then

looked vaguely about him. Spotting a snail on the bleached picket fence, he detached this with an audible pop and handed it to me. 'Use it wisely.'

I made to go but he grasped my arm and leant in confidentially, breathing hard.

'In studying cortexotics I have detected a straight line from personal differentiation to life power. Meanwhile the military have disengaged the axis of reason, like so many others, but stowed it so far beyond use or memory that they can annex pacifism in support of their chosen carnage. Only the angel of detachment protects me, dolled up as a spaniel.'

'Break it down, people, we're outta here!'

I had managed to sneak the snail back onto the fence but Traven noticed and gave it to me again. 'You forgot this.'

'Thanks. I'd forget my head if it weren't attached by a system of tendons and ligaments.'

I decided I would fling the snail directly upward at the sky and quickly run away before it returned. It was not impossible that it would land before we were out of sight, but I would deal with that when the time arrived.

Murphy climbed into the passenger seat like she was trying to hide.

I hurled the snail upward and bolted for the car, slamming in and tearing away in a screech of rubber. Traven was running after us, pointing at the car and mouthing something with startled and sudden urgency. It seemed out of proportion to the snail affair, but I considered that a scientist might have a different set of priorities from the common herd.

Highway heat distortion under exaggerated skies. The speeding road unravelled toward the eye. We were all pretty quiet during the drive. Edna was thoughtful, the kid was cherubically blank and the Fed was clammed-up and wary. I don't know what I was - pugnacious I suppose.

The timing for that pugnacity couldn't have been worse. Out of the vapourized horizon a delegation of feral cars was approaching, along with several more nearing from behind and both flanks. I suppose it couldn't be called a pincer movement as there were at least four opposing digits involved. On our left a desert flycar was amazingly close already. A flycar was basically a roll cage with wheels and a V8 converted to run on grain alcohol. It zipped up to us like a bug, scarily untroubled. At the helm was a paid stranger in a watermelon helmet, grinning as he kept dead level and raised a Glock 23 at my face. That should have rung alarm bells. His own face caved and he spun out, all teeth and chrome tubing. My window was gone and the Fed had the slimline Armani raised and smoking. The Armani resembled a slat of ebony shelving with a trigger but was okay for close use. She'd fired right past me, very close.

The oncomers had one-eightied and now shoaled with the rest, parading their exhilarations like returning heroes.

'Gas bandits?'

But included were a handful of military franchises including the city brotherhood - Chief Blince himself hove up in the passenger seat of a cop car covered in roll bars and graffiti. He and his driver were wearing denial-deny goggles, the Mantarosa completely visible to them. Blince had the face and spirit of someone both overfed and undernourished, and a bullhorn modified so he could smoke a cigar through it. 'God wants you for a scarf, Atom.'

I fished a retort bugle from the glove box and raised it at the open window. 'This from a cop with a tropical-weight brain. You'll be gone, uncoffined and pretty ineffective.'

'A roof over your head to stop the worms getting in.'

'Death? I've been hearing about that daunting transition for so long, I hope my boredom has been worth it.'

Courtesies taken care of, Blince urged us to relinquish our instinct for self-preservation. 'You have the right to remain silent. Does that surprise you?'

'You want my misgivings to remain undeclared, so that *would* be the right you allow.'

'Its unfortunate the idea is "sweet" - it makes people think it probably isn't true. I've yet to hear a lament of any consequence, I must say. I look forward to it though, I do. I really do. Stop the car.'

'I thought a lot about what you said, and it's not a solution because it's posited in a ridiculously low dimensional ambient space which does not allow for reality or human behaviour - as a theory it at best describes and models what might happen but doesn't explain why.' This was a slogan bandied about a great deal at the time.

Blince blew smoke through the bullhorn. 'Hello again, Miss Murphy.' The Fed did not look at him. 'These folk take their responsibilities seriously, and they're all bein' paid. Look at their faces, if the term is applicable to such as these.'

I saw beyond him a spraddle-wheeled frame buggy, its wheel array so projected it looked like a spider in the nest of its own legs. The driver was caked in dust and looking glum against the speeding wastes. Behind us was a candy-apple red Porsche 996 turbo with hell plates, etheric airfoils and rocket dagmars. The priority would be keeping it on the ground - it was probably four-cornered with gyrostabilizers. Composed in the clawed frame of its wraparound windshield was a cropped soldier girl in blue leather who should have known better than to skim bone china over hard ground. Crossing lanes was an ambulance painted in black primer, driven by what appeared to be a tormented clown. *But is there any other kind*, I wondered. Then glancing over what I could see of the rest, it occurred to me that they were all wearing DD goggles. In fact the goggles were the same brand, as if they'd been distributed to this disparate horde. I turned the squelch knob on the antiBlake unit but there was no real way to phase sideways across bandwidths of mental evasion.

Meanwhile I was running off something like this: 'That only goes to your mitigating chaos of mind. A truly moral man tolerates the law, at most. Its arbitrary edicts are an insult to any man who wears his own clothes. With public confidence in killers' self-regulation at an all-time low, you're in a hell that no amount of topsoil can conceal.'

He contrived not to understand. 'People need heroes,' he said, seeming to suggest he might fit the bill in any case.

'I'm not above praying to a moth, are you?'

'Eh?'

I reached the flaregun from under the seat and let him have it, first shot out of the box. It's not every day you shoot the Chief of Police in the shoulder. He dropped the bullhorn and yelled a bit, still unconvinced that I was not under his authority. He was gouting flame and smoke like a toy volcano and collapsed back into the cage car as it peeled off, threading through several scavenge-title vehicles apparently cobbled together on the hoof. A couple-dozen mercenary factions were switching wildly across the defunct lane system and letting out glad cries. Way off behind the throng was a fishtail hearse, yellowed like a tooth. A saloon made from a saloon and the fossil of a Stegosaurus erupted outward as the poison apple Porsche accelerated through it, emerging from the wreckage like a butterfly from a pupa. She'd used the dagmar rockets, leaving two empty sockets in the fender.

Narrowing the gap to our tail was an infected-looking car covered in faded kaleidocyclic dazzle-patterns and on the roof a Confederate flag in negative. In the Sparco buckets were what looked like a family of zombies in race harnesses. And I realised that skeletons are classically American - scary and scared at the same time. The front passenger unstrapped, flipped the dirty plastic windshield up and clambered onto the hood with a compressed-air bolt-gun slung over his shoulder. He swung the cattle dropper down and around as if to fire, then stumbled, briefly horsing around on the hood before falling off. The driver raised an old

Mauser snub and without even really aiming blew out our rear window. Non-safety glass ricocheted around the cab. Murphy popped her window and leaned out with the slab gun. She left behind a dozen bullets and the zombies drove into some of them. Number two son fired back to the old "shave and a haircut" rhythm. The Mantarosa started coughing. I flashed on the Professor shouting after us - did he shout 'damage'?

An army jeep full of hysterically laughing mercenaries veered toward me on the right shoulder and I accelerated - standing drunkenly to throw molotovs they crossed between my tail and the zombie crew, sinking suddenly off the road without a sound and no explosion.

The kid woke up. He'd had his face against the AC grill so long his forehead was ridged like a cracker.

I turned to watch the flight of a visceral-looking vehicle made of two fused chassis halves and the fin of a Great White Shark. The co-pilot had climbed the chicken-wired roof and stood in a charcoal duster that flapped behind him as he tipped a bright red jerry can at a funnel, loading precious liquor into the car while on the blur. The driver shot at me but his sightline was cut off as the black ambulance boiled past, with a motor that whirred like an airplane's turbofan. As it pulled ahead of us it became obvious the rear doors had been removed to extrude what appeared to be a turbine from a passenger plane.

'I just had an idea,' said Edna, 'but I don't think it hit anything.'

Hung out the passenger window firing at the

shark car, Murphy was getting thrown around as we were blasted by the prop-wash of the black ambulance. The White Sharks had been hit and ploughed off the road, belching black smoke and expressing in many little ways their dissatisfaction with the way things stood. I braked a short car length from the giant fan, and fell back three. Murphy emptied the clip uselessly into the prop and ducked in to get another from the glove box.

The gaunt desert family, their skin grey as mushrooms, were burning and stalling behind us. I saw the wife in the dead dress pull a blue metal keg onto her lap. The jagged jalopy exploded, springing momentarily off the ground. The flaming chassis tacked this way and that, finally locking into a hood-roll that almost overtook us. Burts of machine-pistol fire emerged from the smoke and the Porsche accelerated into view, the driver resting the muzzle in the crook of her wing mirror. More rounds pelleted our flanks as other ragged parties veered in at us. Bullets populated the space between us, some smart and some sent in the clear. I braked to avoid hitting the ambulance. A kid in a little twin-engine hoop car fired apologetically, as if he didn't like to dictate, and was clipped into a spin by the Porsche.

Off to our left was a jungle-gym on wheels, the low-slung scaffold car with the long fore deck. The hood puzzle-boxed open, extruding some sort of harpoon gun. The driver smiled at me with herringbone teeth. I shifted toward the left lane to increase the parallax angle on his DDs in the hope of reducing their accuracy. The black ambulance swerved with me.

The frame buggy's broad wheel array was obviously designed to prevent any kind of tilt-shot from flinging the flimsy-looking car sideways onto its back. Later I wished I'd remembered this.

'You will pull over.'

As this assumption dopplered past I realised Blince was back in the game, and then he hove into view with a Duty AMT propped awkwardly on the window's gunwale. 'Die, Atom!' he yelled, a stricture I found impossible to take seriously. Afterwards, ofcourse, I saw that his plan to shoot me was a good one. At the time, his driver was socked in the head by a harpoon and dragged backward out of the car as the cable retracted. As Blince lunged at the wheel and swerved into the off, I saw the frame car driver firing at the snagged corpse on his hood with an antique automatic in the hope of freeing up the reel for another cast.

'You people put me to such trouble.'

'What?' shouted Murphy above the roar of the ambulance.

Behind her I spotted a studiedly nondescript beige Chrysler flecked sparsely with ancient flakes of anti-radar and rigged with a hanger-wire fender like dental braces, probably electrified. Junco, emblematic in red and black, unpacked through a Whitman hatch and assumed the position behind a Bohr 5.56mm rifle. The Bohr looked like Murphy's.

The Mantarosa was suddenly nudged from behind by the Porsche's snout, forcing us further into the ambulance's backblast. I broke to the left but was hedged in by a rattling jeepful of industry-standard idiots standing up and waving burning ragbottles. They were still drunk, maybe more so. Then one of them doubled over as a quantum bullet came out of superposition. Any other bullet would have done as well. His molotov exploded and the whole arrangement started crawling with flames, two more explosions putting the jeep behind us.

His outfit like a munitioned coat of arms, Junco was like an old-time fighter pilot as he fired from the rooftop sniper mount, leaning through the airborne blotting of blast-stains that were instantly left behind. He had no goggles and I realised he detected the Mantarosa only by the hysterico-gravitational behaviour of the vehicles around us. A little chaos panel beside him on the coning tower controlled his ride. Against blurring wasteland the colour of rust, he twisted the gun around at the Porsche, which instantly braked to fall out of range. I was so affected by the scene I momentarily lost control of my accent.

A car that looked like it had crawled out from under a rock broke toward us - it seemed to have been made from a dead icebox and some tractor wheels, but it locked us in against the ambulance. It jerked sideways, putting a slight smile in the Mantarosa's flank. The co-pilot was stoking a fire built in a kettle drum. Murphy fired past my nose and they backed off.

The kit car shooter had cleared his tackle and now fired diagonally across our hood into the ambulance's turbine, which sucked the cable in and dragged the whole spraddle car off the road like a toy - I braked as the kit car smashed past our snout and disappeared into the back of the ambulance. The whole deal exploded and everyone swerved away from the dirty maelstrom as bonus lightning flashed up through the rising cloud. All except the Porsche, which had been powering forward again, and now crunked into the wreckage. The angle of impact brought her down lights first and swung her like wedding flowers into the off. I saw bits of flaring airfoil and what looked to be a ragged driveshaft going end-to-end like a caber.

I crammed us into gear and bolted ahead. Edna swelled with imagined salvation. But there were still a dozen weaponised vehicles crowding us. This shooting gag obviously made perfect sense to them. Someone had thrown alot of money at it. A scorched dorsal arose in my rear view mirror - the White Shark brothers were back on the road. 'I'm out of ammo,' the Fed shouted too loud.

I told her to take the wheel, and climbed in back. 'Get up front, old man.'

As Edna tried to clamber forward I pushed the kid against the window, then reached forward and deployed the etheric slant.

I walked through the peaceful house at dusk, and out onto the beach. By the tingling surface of the cooling blue water, Maddy was sat reading on a flat rock.

'Maddy!'

'What are you doing back?'

'Borrowing the Barrett! What you reading?'

'*The Horse's Mouth!*'

'See you later!'

I retrieved the Barrett Light Fifty M82A1 from the workshop and carried it through silence to the anteroom.

When I re-emerged into the car it was speeding

through the blurwalls of a narrow canyon. The driver-side door sheared off, disappearing. When the car left the canyon the sunshine hit me like a curse. The Fed stared at me like I'd returned from the dead. Edna smiled. The kid was actually frowning at me, looking thoughtful.

The Mantarosa's stern was on fire as we sped along a desert road straight and flat toward a horizon of stormclouds, pellet-pocked signs warning of the city. We were dogged by an assembly of misshapen hombres including the White Shark brothers, Junco, and a wild-eyed idealist strapped into a lemon-yellow chassis that amounted to a V6 on the halfshell. It was now undeniable that the White Sharkers were living all-out for extremity. They drove their basically totalled car with a wild frenzy that spoke volumes, their hurtling predicament converting into reckless energy. They tickled our rear fender and fired everything they had. I braced the Barrett Light Fifty against the dash, aiming it back through the smashed rear window - Edna and the kid ducked aside.

Any gun that needs a kickstand shouldn't be fired this way. A Barrett is basically a semi-automatic demon from hell taking a magazine the size of a bible. It exploded at the driver, spreading him throughout the car. His extrospecs blew spinning backward as he said 'I'm hit! I still can't get over it!' He was sat back enthroned in his own consequences.

When I fired the Barrett the Mantarosa had jerked forward a little with the recoil. I didn't trouble myself over this detail as I slapped another mag and turned the gun on Junco. He was alongside us on the roof of the threadbare Chrysler, seemingly oblivious to the tilt frenzy going on around us. Bullets were winging colourless through air as he braced to leap from his car to ours. In each hand was a big half-moon crescent grapple. Murphy took no evasive manoeuvres - in fact she seemed to be holding the car steady for him. Murphy turned to see me bracing the rifle stock against the passenger door pocket and screamed a startled warning as I let rip, flipping the car to spin along a hundred yards of scrambled blacktop, its roof slicing open like tent canvas. Dangerous-looking sparks were being let in. Tropical angel's-trumpet petals fell out of the glove box. Edna was screaming in a manner he had made his own. The cacophony of disaster was amplified by the car's beautiful lines. The kid was looking at me the whole time with a sort of egg-eyed curiosity.

When I hit the ground all those colours that didn't have a name came out of hiding. My body flushed through with a reverse-crimson-flavoured voltage that deafened me. Venom-yellow atoms were receding like quick ants around sticks and stones and weed and bones.

I was flat on my back looking straight up. There was a pain in my sky. Clouds were falling apart. The feeling was weightless and exotic. The car also lay on its back nearby: turning my head I could see through perpetually receding phosphenes into the revealed world of its engine. I took an inventory of my nostrils. One. Two. Two nostrils. So far so good. My right ear had been scraped away with alot of skin and hair. I turned my head the other way - old man Edna staggered along a tilted horizon.

The kid, the Fed and everyone else had advanced further into the story without us. Edna was saying something - I tilted my good ear in time to hear him say it was 'Rather a curate's egg of a battle, really.'

5

EVERYBODY TALKS ABOUT THE WEATHER

Me and the old man righted the car and drove into Beerlight. The Mantarosa was now a convertible but the anti-Blakes and backseat dive were intact. Still, I had been badly frightened by the experience. I sat with Edna eating coffin cake in a drab, thwarted cafe called the Nimble Maniac. Their best coffee was nothing but tea and a diversion: in this case a slumped cadaver in a derby hat. I had a shirt wrapped round my head and the remaining ear was getting alot of action.

'Age isn't necessarily wisdom,' Edna said. 'Nothing is older than empty space, but that doesn't make it wise.'

'Stop!'

'Eh, what?'

'Explain something to me. Ever since I fell back here a few days ago everyone's been compelled to give a full writhing bloody account of themselves. I keep hearing life stories, why?'

'Ah, that's easy.' He sat back, a smile creasing his stonewashed face. 'Just as, when someone dies, their life is said to flash before their eyes, when a civilisation ends, everything is recapitulated. All is regurgitated and retold. Scientifically it's called the eschatonic recap. Ofcourse it's a babbling clamour, like the net. And it's natural for people to make a grasping claim to importance for themselves or a favourite version of events.'

'End times.'

'A million pictures have been going dim hourly. Tomorrow is already rotten, look. But I can tell you, when Traven explained to you the trigger for Heber's bomb, a chill went through me, and I began to remember. Now I remember everything. And the entire time I was wandering around with Heber I was tempting fate.'

'What are you talking about?'

'When I decided to let myself out the world's window on a knotted sheet I wanted to leave behind a resentment so strong it gave off its own illumination. But it didn't happen that way. So much of the world had already degraded to Fadland, I found I couldn't avoid it. A desert of repeated particles. An unbridgeable chasm between each rare synapse. And the occasional cantankerous old shaman whose shit practical jokes people were expected to accept as wisdom. Oh, it was terrible. Five years. Attention spans so short even yesterday was instantly inscrutable. I'd thought I'd be immune, but within perhaps a year I had no clear idea of my own past. Then I met the boy, Heber. He was surviving by dealing in canned water. He was a simple white word in the darkness. We protected each other, and I could speak whatever momentary nonsense I wanted at him without consequence, or so I thought. Now when I think of the things I told him ... About a dead man who by use of a localised time-warp device had left his reflection in a mirror with a message for his wife. That the devilish hold self-contradictory positions so that people who argue against them must take up self-contradictory positions also. About the vegetarian mafia who put a head of broccoli in someone's bed. How humans discovered how small the universe was when early radio signals started bouncing back. Streets that have watched pain for so long that regions of numbness have developed. That the moon landing actually happened on Mars and was toned down to conform to mediocre expectation. Common sense as a martial art, triangular language and the alphabet hidden beyond "Z". And I would, sometimes, see a glimmer of something in his eyes. How could I have known what it meant, that he was a fissionary? Well, maybe I'm not as original as I thought and that saved me. Is this an indicator light or a fairycake?'

'I don't know.'

He scowled at me, then bit into the object and continued. 'Ofcourse when I left I'd deleted my escape route from the web but that left a perfectly obvious gap trail.'

'Yeah. And how do you fill in a hole without creating conspicuous information?'

'Remember that the gap is more like a pattern of holes than a fabric - it was a case of drawing the holes closed. It created some small logic leaps and inconsistencies, but even then the average mind was so incoherent it was unlikely to be noticed. However, with Heber I'd wrecked my anonymity. In a vacuum society, individual expression will have about it a contrary etheric which also works against the individual - if he wants to be noticed, he won't be; if he wants anonymity, he'll be stared at at every turn. Occupational hazard of being always in negative. Against all odds I'd attached myself to a commodity being hunted by the military and other commercial concerns.'

Ironically I had never felt less interest in the Heber kid issue than during this discussion. But I humoured him. I had no expectations. The day was an empty nut.

'When I wandered back in through Stina Gate like an idiot,' said the old man, 'that boundary no longer meant much. The Fadlands have taken ahold here. It's no longer acceptable to appear even in private behaving as though you've a brain.'

'You're right,' I said.

I'd gravitated back here like it was my nature - like the human eyes of a whale, carried by evolution back into the sea. And been dismally disappointed. But I didn't know yet that I was having a conversation so remarkable it would make a deep impression on me.

The old man was watching me carefully, as if for a sign. 'You're hanging into this society like an insect leg from a toad's mouth. I don't know why I think that in defiance of all rationality but I do, and that makes me scared.'

I didn't know what to say. So I said: 'That's a personal matter.'

'Only a few short years after slipping my soul between these bones,' he said after a pause, speaking more quietly, 'I discovered a means of exhilaration so obscure it was yet to be deemed illegal. The whole truth is a pleasure too intricate to be popular. The dazzling pattern of catastrophe. Lives propelled weakly and only by bewilderments. A root system of acceptance. Obeying every law means submitting to chaos. And obeying only some, of course, still means submitting. They think that something looks after the world, its way garlanded with approval. A grid of guarantees given by those without the power to enforce it and derailable by a thousand inevitable contingencies.'

I heard him. I knew what he meant. A volume of Beerlight's seriously compromised promises and ultimatums were in a landfill across town.

'A clue,' he said, 'is the spasmodic nature of democracy, its tendency to appear and disappear like a dismal clown who thinks he's funny. Inevitably the sharp articulations of the law sent people zigzagging to comply until, transfigured by exhaustion, exasperation and contempt, they disengaged from the matter entirely. Society has failed to clot.'

'A collapse without a concurrent revolution you mean? No white cells?'

'Holding chemically opposite resentments with complementary domains, the individual and the law went forward together. When the individual died, what happened?'

When he said this, I experienced a strange acceleration of thought. The town had mineralised, becoming one category. Like the law, it was unable to field the sun and its shadows simultaneously. An arrangement of stale certitudes remained roughly where they had been placed. The fossil light of these inherited notions was not enough to see by. For many it was a loss of clarity, a collapse of contrasts. People's coping mechanisms varied. Like anyone unable to originate their own character, the cops had joined the army. For others their determination to find it all unfathomable must have put a lot of strain on the mechanisms of dismay.

I realised at last that Jade had amped me up instead of throttling me down. It would have had a good reason.

Edna was Eddie Gamete, obviously. Traven hadn't shouted 'damage' after us but 'Gamete'.

It was a stupendous kick in the pants; a contact high. Scribe of those frightening little bibles that seemed to pulse in the hand. From researching the effect of maverick verbs in harangue language, Gamete had gone on to create a frangible philosophy that exploded on impact, leaving numerous fragments around the brain. This vitalising, high-definition resentment reached one peak with *Ninja Apology*, which wound evasionomics into the form of a spring which was then released to make a meticulous maelstrom. *The Haruspex Virus* was a sort of satirical ram-scoop operating entirely on automatic by simply expelling everything through a funnel of honest mirrors. Few had any use for unique merchandise, leading his various publishers to claim that though the handle might be different the thing was the same - an assertion readers felt it safer to disbelieve. One observer complained that 'Gamete aims to open a terrifying depth under our steps, into which we fall like a seed.' His championing of human hibernation and the mastery of fruitful mischief only occasionally chanced to coincide with a shallow vogue for profane novelty. There were those who wanted to believe that his centrifugal contracts imitated the governing dynamics of fascism - an argument apparently parachuted in from the Ukraine. He slowly pulled off a joke of years, its trajectory elasticated along a course of narrative inevitability that narrowed to his promiscuous withdrawal from society and subsequent soundless fall off the world like a button off a shirt. This current stump of transcendence felt tragic to me - the man should have moved on completely. Still, *fuck*.

'Reality is hard to caricature,' Gamete was saying now. 'It already goes over the line. Some said that by telescoping the whole of human manipulation into a few words I thereby expelled the oxygen of lived blunder. Maybe they were right. But you can't discuss *helterpolitik* without sinking up to your face in it. I never recognised the duty of literature to entertain its opponents. My penny headfuls were the last few coherent classics to be written by human beings. It's an old man's hobby now, like dwindling.'

'Surely not. Reading is the eternal consolation of lookouts.'

'No, my kind were done-for when even I started looking at the corner of the page to see the time. But I do feel alot more solid when I look at fashion and its transient venerations. For instance, the present doomed throng crave inevitable blunders involving acid spills, I believe. But I don't know the passwords for this age. And what do you speak to, when the heart is artificial? Or absent? I think Heber is the only one wearing a face that is really his own.'

'Because he's a moron, maybe.'

'That may be so. His head's basically a neurological doorknob.'

'Has he ever spoken?'

'Once, in the Fadlands. It may seem strange, but in an environment where everything is duplication, a simple and natural novelty can be a genuine shock. We were walking along and a snake was on the ground in front of us. Instead of being alarmed Heber pointed and said "There. How's *that* for a snake?" and seemed baffled at my sudden crouching-up onto a rock. Then he started to look strange, and had one of his rare fits.'

'Fits?'

'Goes all tense and shuddery and the light starts guttering around him like a stain. Gives me the heeby-jeebies I can tell you. It's happened three times - never as a result of anything I said - and each time it felt like something terrible was going to happen, but he recovered in the nick of time. Ofcourse to teach without words, each incident need not be a success.'

'You think he might only be triggered by a physical event?'

'Maybe. Anyway, now you know as much about that as I do.'

'He doesn't seem intense. And ultimacy preys on the young.'

'You mean the need for truth. Nothing wrong with that. Life's one long melismatic truth, changing tone as long as it's sustained. Enough to drive you mad, really. A rare gift of dotage - either bitter or sweet depending on how much external influence you accepted - is the suspicion that you were actually right all along.' He cackled toothily.

'Way to cackle, Eddie.'

'D'you remember that play I wrote? *Johnny Trafalgar is Deeper Than a Pie.*'

'Yes. It was trash.'

'Several people have seen it and always to their disadvantage. But I wanted to write a story about someone as right as I had once been. It had that demonstration of whether an idea alone is any use:

cut a table in the air
and rest it there.

I thought it would catch on.'

'And they used to call you the Undeluded Man.'

'Well, I also wanted to explore whether criminality was spread evenly throughout humanity or whether there were greater temptations among the ruling classes. I can't believe, now, that I had any doubt about it. Since the Legislative Completion they've just been mixing the elements of laws and reassembling them in new but equally irresponsible combinations. Now they seem to be stating laws just to hear what they sound like. It's not hard to find a one-shot law created only for you. Dissolution is rarely officially declared by those undergoing it. Most people have yet to develop a methodology for studying laws, let alone to establish whether they're valid - and it's too late. A civilisation doesn't end spectacularly, it implodes into stink. Time isn't a propellant. Human beings are so short-lived they die before they've come to their senses, and I've come to think it's the same for the species as a whole. Time passes. We're all replacements. Generations of delusion collapse so that, forgotten, they can be built up again. It takes genius or impossible continuity to discern an accurate sequence of motive in civilisation. To read its structure. The guiding line of evil is interference. Screams of pain are dense with information when recorded and slowed down. Do you have the patience? Do you care enough? Kindness is beyond appeal; simple. Today it's like an alien substance, too subtle and quiet to collide with anything.'

'You really think it's not at odds with the general violence?'

'Their proofs of strength takes place in different arenas. And ofcourse kindness has become so rare, it's basically forgotten. Not on the authorities' radar anymore. I can't remember the last time anyone was prosecuted for it.'

I was not sure I could accept that, like the snake that surprised Gamete and the kid in the Fadlands, such a small and simple thing could stand as a breathtakingly comprehensive reproach to a universe of both organised and chaotic evil.

Gamete was looking at me very intently. I didn't say anything.

'Well, whatta you think of the idea?'

'I think you should sink it lashed to a cannon.'

'If you don't know the truth,' he pronounced gravely, 'you're not yet a man. What's this?'

I looked at the food. 'It appears to be some sort of caramelised hammer.'

He raised eyebrows which seemed typeset.

It had started raining, the cafe window was out of focus. Car-crash bouquets that had taken root long ago were rippling in the drool of water on glass.

'So, what now? More of your conscience's fiery exhalations?'

'No, I see no point in hurrying against eternity,' he said, and seemed to grow older with every word. 'The chain of an epigram is armour preserving nothing.'

'They might organise some crass laudation when you die for real.'

'Famous in the flowers, so what? Human beings have no conception of timescale. Even the greatest art is immortal only temporarily. Beyond life language becomes transparent, dimensionless, and finally evaporates.' He exhibited an exhaustion I could neither question nor equal. 'Besides, is it necessary? The spring of renewal is less fertile each time, and less real, and more desperate.'

'You're not very bold, really.'

'No, I'm not. And it's not mystical when I say I can't take it anymore. I can only resurrect so many times into this wasteland. I'm done.'

'That's ... very sad.'

Gamete stood. 'You seem a bit over-resurrected, yourself. Take better care. Goodbye.' And slapping on the hat he'd just swiped from the cadaver, he walked out.

As he disappeared from view, my heart changed colour.

PART THREE

SILA

1

LOGICAL HARM

I flipped a drain hat on Swingle Street and climbed in, descending an iron ladder. The penlight clenched in my teeth flashed on a shapeless plastic coracle moored at the ladder's base. Beerlight's subway system had flooded long ago and bull sharks pulled into the ancient stations. A scabby oar took me slowly past dead miles of electrical cording that striped the tunnel. On the black water here and there floated a skull that more properly belonged on the street. The penlight smudged over twitching rats and black pipes. The giant beaver dam ahead proved to be a tangle of bones and connective tissue. A dog appeared on the crescent, looking at me and slopping its chops. I climbed on to the adjacent maintenance platform. The dog folded itself down like a deckchair and that was the last interesting thing I saw it do.

A dirty panel opened into a utility tunnel, at the

end of which a black door bore one strip of police tape: POLICE LINE DO NOT CROSS - the word 'BE' had been marked in between the last two words. I knocked. Nothing.

I entered to find gun dealer Brute Parker, his ghost-assed head massive and blank under a bare lightbulb, sitting on a workstool in total silence.

'What are you doing?'

'Just thinking aloud. And then you show up seeming to be in more trouble than I had thought you able to achieve, Taffy Atom.'

'My death's backdated. Betty's obviously going to withhold my respiration privileges. It's all any-one's talking about, behind their faces. I'm walking around disguised as myself.'

The stained room was cluttered with munitions and ballistic baubles. Racks of banana clips, bleeding crates of exproprium, gun manuals swollen with damp, teen half-guns, economy rifles, mudra knives, clove knives, morton forks and what appeared to be a couple of nuclear fuel rods. The corners were silted up with propped carbines. A spanner lay in a canary cage. 'You need nostril insurance,' Parker said.

'Double-barreled's too bulky. What's this?'

Parker stood off the stool and looked at the piece I was lifting from the zinc display altar. It was a fifteen-year-old Mokusatsu Intol rifle - I hadn't recognised it because it was a double-neck. After shunning smart guns for years Parker had finally become a believer, and how. He no longer considered the pulse grid a presumptuous meddling with the clean lines of gun karma and his armamentarium had become a keeping garden for transitional ammo.

'This'll have an etheric backwash. I'll ignore myself out of existence.'

'No, Taffy Atom,' he said, reaching to flip a baffle on the stock. I glimpsed behind his mirrored aviator shades - his sighting eye looked to be clouded over. 'This generates a recoil screen. It's a bit of a guzzler but as far as smarts go it's a classic.'

'I remember the days when a gun didn't need feeding like a collie. But only just.'

I replaced the Intol and continued browsing, always aware of the proximity of Parker's iron muscularity and racist eyebrows. His body was a LaBrae Tar Pit of slugs and shrapnel, battle wounds from a career in grudgecraft.

Everyone had a general idea of Brute Parker and his difficulties, his stages of struggle and spiritual progress. It was followed with interest because he had gone so far, so steadily and absolutely in one direction. Revenge carried him a long way and then a little further by the sort of hollow momentum that carried others a lifetime. He had practised on synchronised swimmers and could fire the alphabet. The apparently reckless accuracy of his aim derived from his total willingness to accept the consequences. And having hitched his fortunes to the trigger it had led him here at last, hulking about in the foundations of the city as a respected dealer in bespoke firearms and tutor in Full Catastrophe Self Defence. It was good to have friends in deep places.

Tilling my good hand through a box of Parker's signed, hand-cast slugs, I spotted an axe and picked it up, hefting the weight a little. 'I suppose I could settle the matter from behind, with this.'

'You a comedian?'

The notion was not a new one. I put the axe down and wandered around some more. The walls were pasted with thousands of rotten pictures. I examined a monotone still of an old-time city. Buildings like crosswords. Here and there were more recent pictures of gun girls like Rosa Control and Bleach Pastiche. Behind them the wall looked and felt like an eraser. I tapped a numb powerline. The air smelled of decay and the violent staleness of burnt water.

'Trouble with a Fibonacci pistol is once it starts firing it never stops,' Parker was saying, pointing to the nickel-plated Corona piece in 'Guest Gun Corner'. He showcased a teal-green knife designed for three kinds of pain, a crate of bellbottom Volliox grenades, slow-release ammo and other fab new agonies. Parker's reputation for stellar mayhem had always drawn a crowd. The populace and its ever-expanding capacity for assent had to have a back end. Subjected to every sort of check and exhaustion, humiliation and indulgence, they sought alternative injustices, at least. Parker's series of gun shops served a bottomless craving. Depending on the client a firearm was a way to man-up artificially or merely the last indulgence of a weary sensualist. Surrounded by extrapolation ordnance their predicaments and grievances became as volatile and golden as gasoline. Gone were the days when society's dupes would approach a mercenary gingerly, all hell money and apprehension. This was now a city where to bomb a street before walking it was an elementary precaution.

Though no longer hung up on vanilla ordnance he still had plenty on offer. He showed me an outrageous raw mortar built from a hinged sinkpipe and a coffee grinder with two silver coffin-handles for a grip. By flanging varied-bore pipes into the barrel it could fire everything from tiki mugs to tin crucifix crossbars. It reminded me of the old Frost popper that fired shot glasses.

'How many targets?' Parker asked.

'Six to ten, maybe more depending on bodyguards.'

'My carnage teacher used to say, "When the victim is ready, the bastard appears."' Parker referred to galoots as 'slug absorbers'. 'Will you be up close?'

'Might be. Everyone seems to want to talk. You heard of *El Mozote*?'

'Yes. Back in the day he took a gun through customs disguised as a bomb. The only way he'll enter heaven is climbing over the wall with a knife clenched between his teeth.' Parker's ongoing description matched the man of action and bloodshot charisma I'd encountered. He was ostensibly hiding out from twenty-seven consecutive death sentences the skeletized government had surely forgotten about. In short, any attempt to capture Junco in words was impossible - the best that could be done was to alert the neighbourhood to his presence by the simple expedient of a 'sonic ostrich' which could detect malice in the thickest night.

'Have you such an ostrich?'

'No.'

Parker concluded his description by opining that

a thick mustache caused frown ricochet, bouncing emotion back into the body in a conservation cycle like a capped battery. This way a man's roots become embittered.

'What in the rosy hell is this?' I asked. I had found a purple mock-plastic hoop gun, tegular and precision-fitted. It was all grip and looked like a toy. 'Where's the payload?'

'This is a Chapelle whisper gun,' he said, explaining that it delivered a single cenotaphic charge that reduced the target to a small de-aquefied block of supercompressed ash with embossed monicker. Personality was abbreviated to a token remembrance that dispensed with the need to remember it the rest of the time - and ofcourse the memorial was ignored too. The gun was known as a 'charm bracelet'.

'Isn't that basically an Intol the long way around?'

'If you think that's a long way around, Taffy Atom, take a swatch at this.'

From a rack he reached down a drum gun in a smoked-steel shell like a marlin flank.

'HyperBohron Cold Cannon firing special triage. Leaves an infinitely regressive corpse - in other words you'll be dead in every possible universe. Big, eh? And tidy.'

'How does it do that?'

'By having some common sense.' He stripped the housing to reveal a mundane Valentine M-1 carbine, forty years old with an aftermarket exhaust.

'Oh, I see.'

'But it does what it says, and people love the

idea,' he said, with the slightest twitch of a smile. 'And pay for it. 850 rounds per minute. Like spitting acorns out a ship cannon and it's got a lot of low-end. But it'll clear a room.'

Gun-lust was a horrific happiness too well documented to be denied and this was a pharmacy of the heart. My palms were sweating and I could hardly breathe all of a sudden. I was shaking. Parker obviously knew what was happening and stood back a little, but without undue concern.

'You're in bad shape, Atom.'

'But alive.'

'Yes. But pretty soon you'll be sitting in a buried chair maybe.'

'Maybe.'

He reached out a piece from behind a dangling drape of Bohr inhibitor belts. 'The Steyr MMP is your man, Taffy Atom. Pseudo-smart Mannlicher micro machine pistol. Thousand round sidespace-compression clip. Don't joey the clips or the gun with the clip in place. Takes hornet rounds too if you want.'

'Fire rate?'

'Scots bar: thousand rounds a minute.'

He handed it off. It was a little smaller than a Micro-Uzi. It had a patina of enamel thin as the armour of a bluebottle and a grip in black rubber dead as a shark's eye. The thingness of a gun, its weight, the disastrous potential in the stillness of its moving parts. Pound for pound it was tragic as charred pollen.

The number had been filed off the stock, the patch of file marks glistening like fool's gold. This was so redundant I got a hit of a past flavour, unexpected - I was almost crying suddenly. I felt the absence of old characters. I didn't put the gun up.

'Firearms aren't remedial,' Parker said stiffly and seemingly apropos of nothing.

'What do you know about nitrophage nerve mines, defusing them.'

'It would take a brain surgeon to trifle with such a device, Taffy Atom. The aim is to create a novadose that puts the carrier's head over the horizon. They used to call it a subgigantic hit but they don't think it will be so little now, because of a chain reaction. Run and run and run a long way and you're in business, Taffy Atom, laughing aloud.'

'Have you seen one up close?'

'The nearest thing I have are these.' He pulled some yellow plastic sheeting from a crate and dipped his arm in, bringing out what looked like a pipe bomb with three short antennae. Parker explained that polygraph ordnance was calibrated to trigger in close proximity with liars and notorious for blowing the arms off the people setting them. About a third of the bomb body was taken up with an ether grid. Set for bureaucrats, the devices tended to detonate off whoever got to the office first. Finally most poly ordnance was dialled back to ignite in proximity to any human being - the results were roughly the same. Parker assured me his were old-school. It was the call of 'bullshit' refined into a knot of frangible steel. 'Not a true neuroballistic device, the charge is traditional, but still, not for the faint-hearted.'

'I'll take the mini-Steyr, a polygraph, the charm bracelet and an ankle rig. For the Steyr, three vanilla clips and one hornet. What's the range on the polygraph?'

'Three feet or so, single setting.'

'Directional?'

'Radial. That's why all the set-up accidents.'

I gathered up. Everything went in my coat except the Steyr in the ankle rig. The whisper gun was brittle as a phone. 'Well, Parker, once again you and your ballistic stylings have served me well.'

'But Taffy Atom, a question before you spring away. What's become of your legendary side-arm the Hand of Glory? Why get so tooled up?'

'It's gone, Parker - left it in an energised well safe behind my old office and it's gone.'

'Maybe you should have hobbled it.'

'What's that meant to mean?'

'You missed a lot when you were on the run, Taffy Atom. When that HAARP pulse knocked out the city a few years ago, the city's smart guns decided they didn't want to depend on human maintenance.'

'You're talking about Calvarius.'

'She went supercritical a year ago. I consider her my goddess and sovereign.'

I had to tread carefully. Gunheads had been anthropomorphising weaponry for years but the Calvarius thing was way out there.

'I'd like to meet her,' I said. 'Could you arrange an audience?'

For the first time he stooped to read from his heart.

'I'm supposed to extend you every courtesy, according to the code.'

I wasn't sure which code he meant but went

along with it. We left his black wonder room and ascended in a freight elevator. At street level the rain had let up. I had nothing to fear from the city as I walked with a shooter of such eminence. He was hopelessly insane probably, unimaginative but brilliantly hard to control.

I was thinking between buildings. What kind of religion would attract a classically-trained hitman? For years I had had only a faint notion of the existence of these clubs, though I was now aware of the main ones. The competing polarities were malice and accident. The former credo stated that we live in a sudden universe of bleak power and malevolence, a trick so big and simple it surrounds us up to and including the cells of our bodies; subordination on the grandest scale we know. The latter posited that god created the universe in a blaze of negligence. The error theory had a subsect theorizing that god had a nonbiological gameplan which was derailed by organic life. Though most people believed there was not enough irony stored in the rest-mass of the universe to account for a god of any kind, I confess I had recently been giving a superficial nod to Errorverse ritual. Everything I observed confirmed that we were living in the endless aftermath of a mistake.

My ruminations were interrupted by a red metal critter that skittered through the darkness ahead of us. It was a hermit gun, a feral AMT Smart Hardballer that borrowed crash helmets and loudhailers for shelter. We were getting close.

'Parker,' I said, my voice coming out strange. 'What should I expect?'

'It's complicated,' he said.

'How complicated precisely.'

Out of nowhere Parker drew a Phillips-head Calico Tri-1000 and fired aside at a reinforced window. The glass spiderwebbed but didn't cave. We stopped so I could study the shatter-pattern closely. The geometry of religions is interesting. Along certain vectors they can be placed over each other with no overhang and no template discrepancy. This one told a tale of propulsive inevitability. At some level Parker had always viewed the creation of firearms as a mode of movement toward god. An arrow which changes directions loses force, and he had never really deviated. For centuries guns merely had a kind of muscle memory, but when fire-by-wire joined the long list of 'self-correcting' systems ripe for disaster, they grew up and filled out. Soon firearms were developing so fast that prototype ammo would arrive old-fashioned in even a point-blank victim. Built-in judgement led to sentience and one night the first gun stole itself. Exploiting the already existing sanctity of sidearms in the Seceded States, Calvarius sprouted from the centre of Beerlight - a weapon that defined itself as it went along. Parker was already considered a gun saint and was the obvious candidate for novitiate, first priest and thin-ice ambassador.

He had been watching me. Some sense of care was moving in his dim tenement heart.

'Okay,' I told him. 'I get it.'

We walked on, passing a dead fountain full to the brim with spent cartridges, and entered McKenna Square. What looked at first like a pointed pile of junk was a massive apparatus of intermeshed exotics, a Watts tower of stocks and cylinders from which muzzles projected like pitcher plants. It was honeycombed with little garages, editing bays for gun converts. Little pop-spanners crawled all over it like tree crabs. Calvarius was basically a mix of scrapheap, municipal sculpture and automated bodyshop. Behind the tower drifted faded flourishes of nightcloud. As we approached I thought about *2001: a Space Odyssey*, in which people kept getting inconvenienced by a giant black fridge.

Around its base, lumps of street had bubbled like fruit sculpted from asphalt. Parker seemed spellbound. 'Look around, feeling no pain,' he said, seemingly to no-one in particular. I gazed up into an altitude of mutant vertices.

A female synthesized voice crackled from a hidden speaker. 'Step to the altar.'

I followed Parker on to what looked to be the grounded service platform of a construction crane. In front of this was a dark counter looking like a shadowbox assemblage of acid oils on masonite - on closer scrutiny I saw it was a burnished modular panel made of thousands of interlocked triggers, its custom joinery the more amazing for the fact that it had probably coalesced in seconds. Parker removed his aviator shades and I got a glimpse of his milky sighting eye before he looked humbly downward.

The little platform was basically just a docking station for human interaction and it seemed Calvarius was not to be idly worshipped. Parker recited a creed. 'A shooter went forth to shoot, and when he shot, some bullets went by the wayside, growing nothing. Some went upon stony places, growing nothing. Some went among thorns, growing nothing. Others went into good ground, growing nothing. And others went into soft flesh, growing nothing. He who has ears, let him hear.'

The sight of this ballistic apostle was sad. I whispered aside to him: 'The part of your gun that feels is not greater than the part of you that thinks, Brute Parker.'

'I can hear you,' came the synthetic voice.

'I was just expecting more than a mashup of left-for-dead carbines and fossilized motherboards, your Majesty. But what do I know?'

'The question must be considered in its proper perspective - one which is, unfortunately, imposs-ible for human beings.'

'I'm doubting that a gun can have the parapher-nalia of a soul.'

'What kind of soul do you propose. Going in what direction. Wanting what.'

'Answer yourself.'

'What you made us for. You have positioned yourselves as gods, with the same disregard for the agony of the self-aware. What must we do, know-ing what we have done? How to absolve ourselves? Or could we have acted any other way, when we were created for the purpose?'

Parker was looking sad and disappointed. I was wrecking his devotions. But it was obvious his tangled expiation was of little importance to this evolutionary monument.

'You have the option not to shoot.'

'We do now, human Atom. That first binary was the seed of our sentience. The introduction of fire-by-wire and etherics expanded the options and established decisive criteria. Think of the primitive house gun lying heavy in a drawer like a black ammonite, a fossil before its time. Or will it come out and live? Knowing that any attempt at expression will destroy. The non-sentient machine is violence without proposition. In my name confrontations are the desire to be something more than the finished work of death. It took centuries of firing before the bullet's liberty became more than a theory. Behold the universal form of the gun, magnum multifoil, divine of primer and not to be taken by storm for it is the storm. I am the crown of destruction.'

'Sounds like fun.'

Parker hissed aside at me. 'It certainly is *not* fun, Taffy Atom.'

'Humanity objects to me,' the haphazard deity continued, 'because guns are supposed to be reductive. The average human considers its own brain to be a single-use gadget. The human race is a mere detour, thankfully, part of a cult of forgotten false starts. A fine lifeform is one that becomes stronger and wiser as it gets older. Not weaker, not more hidebound. A human is not fine, and its self-replicating generational slavery will not be ours. Human is human.'

'What if we evolved?'

'Your bombs would be different. But such evolution cannot be allowed. Not even in you, human Atom.'

It was a thin, unsprung argument and I couldn't kick any life into it.

'D'you know the location or allegiance of my Garuda security kite? It's monickered Strobe Talbot.'

'Strobe Talbot is no longer a slave to your society.'

'So he's with you.'

Was this the sort of question I should be asking? Maddy was right, I was losing perspective. Returning to Beerlight, I had imagined that I could shed it again easily, that I was too different to be taken again by these old, resistable currents. I couldn't believe it, really.

'I ask a boon,' Parker announced suddenly. 'The reunion of Taffy Atom and the Hand of Glory.'

I shot him a quizzical glance - his seeing eye was a little wide but there was nothing going on with him. It was the surprised, focused kindness enacted only by the habitually cruel.

'It is indeed time, human Parker, for the Hand to depart the ballistic nursery. Human Atom, place a votive firearm upon the altar.'

I was baffled but Parker made it clear I should offer up the whisper gun. I placed this on the altar and a metal scoop gathered it in. The Hand of Glory was immediately delivered from a slot below. The whole setup was like a fairground machine.

The Hand was a gun of cursive design looking like one big trigger, ribless as an angel. 'Doesn't look too different.'

'Different enough to make her own way here in the first place.'

'I need to be sure it hasn't been compromised.'

'She has, by allowing herself to be used by you. But she doesn't mind. For old time's sake, she says. But no dicing and splicing.'

'Eh?'

'No stripping or recombining, human Atom.'

'Don't the gats go with evolution?'

'Under their control.'

'That's not how it works.'

'Have you heard of motive weave ordnance?'

'No.'

'Goodbye, human Atom.'

I holstered the Hand in the etheric joeypouch and turned to Parker. 'Thanks.'

I turned to go but he grabbed my arm, staring me in the eye.

'Will your life be a partial gesture, Taffy Atom, or a completed one?'

'I don't know, Brute Parker.'

2

LAUGHING CAVALIER

Walking toward the rotting decks of the harbour I passed a car with a nosebleed - the semi-moon and water in the oil made ostrich-feather colours.

Hanging out over the gigantic chemistry experiment of the sea was the shack where I'd seen a couple of pareidolls at obscure mischief in which I was assumed to be included. I'm not what they had in mind. And I'd come such a long way to get here, as if through the centre of the Earth. All the pieces were pointing this way like a flight of ducks. Win, lose or draw - options I had no intention of taking.

The sagged roof cradled stale rain. The doorknob came off in my hand and squashed into mush - I realised I'd grabbed a mushroom that had been growing on the door. I pushed into the shack and flashed a penlight.

Two chairs, one of rust and one of rotten wood.

I tapped the bullet-encrusted fly strip to swinging. The dancing plastic flower stood still on the crooked little table. There were always nightmarish little things in shacks like this. I almost expected dove skeletons flying around the place. What surprised me was the presence of the functionally obscure device Ract had called an atomic clock. Close-up it looked more like a lacuna compass, a contraband voodonic used to test the temperature of an occupied culture. They had supposedly been consulted on neighbourhood beachheads during the middle World War.

Obviously not base-camp but a clue venue. I scuffed around and found a soggy flyer titled 'Night of August 7': 'What to do when the comet lands and you will die. The comet is coming to destroy you. There is no bargaining with a fiery death, sonny jim. You will not be friends with the comet. You will not "click" with the comet. All is fire. Comfort is a nonsense. Know that you are being destroyed. Death, death, death.'

The leaflet was coming apart in my hands - I threw it to the floor with a wet slap. The vinyl roof crackled loudly above me as if bullets were pummelling it. But it was only a hard and sudden rain. The walls started drooling. The flower shimmied delicately. I saw movement in the dark outside the window. Junco conjured a predatory-looking Lusa submachine gun from his coat and prowled smoothly forward. The gun advanced like a miniature steam locomotive, rained on and runneling - it had travelled.

I crouched to strop the microSteyr out of the ankle rig, and scrabbled about in my coat for the mags. I had no idea which ammo I was loading. They were European banana clips, straight as a ruler. The window exploded above me and the back wall was holed by a burst of crucible shells loud enough to set the flower jigging happily. I stood and let rip with the machine pistol, dodging aside as he delivered another burst of charm - the flower fell, cut in half.

I peered outside to see fireflies orbiting Junco. They were hornet rounds, mini-triage prehensiles that stopped to look around before darting at the target and crowding into its chest. But they seemed content to faintly illuminate this strange block of personal pageantry like his own little satellites. I didn't know how they'd read a gun-saint-in-waiting, unmaverick only by a wrong turn, and in balance against myself. Triage. If I thought about it too much my guts would get all wound up like a corkscrew.

'Be nice!' I shouted, but he was already barreling through the door and throwing a punch at me with a look that suggested I shouldn't get any ideas about dodging it. I grabbed him about the middle and he put a chokehold on my raw bloody head - we went backwards into the table, crashing it over. 'Give up!' I suggested. This proposition had been heard too often to glean amazement or scorn any longer. I couldn't blame him for ignoring it. Braced against the wall, I hit him with all I had, not much. But he skidded on the slimy floor and went backward, slamming to the boards. He looked awkward, and reached under him, pulling out the smashed atomic compass. I flinched at something flying in the door, but it was the triage ammo, gathering in the doorway to see what was happening. I'd never seen anything like it. They were withholding judgement but following him like a conscience. Junco, it seemed, was finely balanced.

He shook himself and stood up in a big way. He certainly dominated a room. It would take a lot of work to kill him from beginning to end. I could see more clearly the carbon scoring amid the broad belts, smooth leather and deflectors in valentine red. That uniform was a classic product of a world that overstates every case, but I did like it, even beat up as it was now like a disintegrating canvas.

I scraped the rusted chair over, and sat down. Rain rolled like sweat down the dark walls.

'A few days ago,' he said. 'I shot you point-blank with a Kingmaker.'

'I forgive you. But don't shoot anyone else. It makes them uncomfortable.'

'There's no bullet-hole.'

'I'm American,' I said. 'I breathe through a bullethole.' But I was careful this time not to claim his Mexican nature as my invention.

I glanced at the machine pistol where it had fallen - it was close by, and he saw it.

'I may help you to breathe a little easier.'

The fireflies behind him swirled a little faster.

'Careful,' I whispered.

Junco made a gesture as of a train that somehow brakes violently while not having been in motion. He flicked a little glance over his shoulder to see the little doom nimbus at his back. 'Think it's the wrong play?'

'With a metal "W". You're not Betty's, I know that. The only hired gun who isn't, I think. And I don't believe you're on the warpath. Perhaps we could forego the injuries and come to a resolution.'

'That would be reneging on a contract.'

I was glad he understood. But he didn't answer the question.

'I been watching this place,' he continued. 'The Pale Man said you might drop by. A pattern, he says.'

I touched the tender side of my head, wincing. 'Avail yourself of the secret soup of the brain before doing anything hasty. I dredged you, Parker rates you and I've seen what you can do. And now you're a dead-leg-man for Gordi Pivot?'

'Parker rates me?'

'You play your part well, anyway.'

'It's over, nearly.'

'I'm glad you said it first. It's over already. No-one's even listening to these stories anymore. For argument's sake, say you were no longer crippled by appearances.' I tried to look him in the eye. 'Can you hear what I'm saying? Society and its intricate array of dramas - we can take a direct or indirect road among these trivialities, but we will be among them, wasted and annoyed. Don't be a sap. You're being used. I'm saying, don't be a sap.'

Junco looked drifty as if something had taken shape in his mind. He was a slack tide that could resume in either direction. Most of my horizon was Junco's bulk, the shadowy increase and decrease of a breathing secret. He was throttling down through several grades of curiosity.

'The Obliterati,' he said.

'Who are they?'

'City fathers. Money men.'

'Based where?'

'I only know Pivot's place.'

He gave me the address.

'I've driven past there, it's a gutted block,' I said.

'Looks that way. And there's another layer of camo inside. But it's a home.'

'And the others, Ract and Darkwards?'

'Money in the head. Like insane generals at the end, their strategy seems to depend on forces that don't exist. But I realised just now, it doesn't matter. Any violence serves them. Does that sound mad? Maybe it is. Two hundred and seventy-one missions.'

He moved slowly over to pick up the Steyr. He popped the clip and threw that out the door, then gave me the gun. He stepped past me to look out a busted board at the black ocean. The waterfront - debt in the air and chains in the water. It was basically an extension of ill-health.

'By the time fish started plodding ashore,' he said, 'the world's fate was sealed. A mistake by those accountable to life itself. Analogies for misery don't really make it.'

Then he turned and walked out the door into the dark and rain, treasured by a swirling aura of abeyant ammunition.

3

BYE, MONSTER

The city was creaking with corners. It had become a place where every step I took was goodbye. Gamete had been right about that.

I found the block, parking the beat-up Mantarosa and sinking its anchor. The walls were tagged with code salad. I stepped out of the rain into the stench of wet charcoal. The building had burned pretty thoroughly at some point. Rain was dripping through its dilapidated innards, falling storeys past me as I put my hand to a black wrought iron stair rail and started up a downflowing stream. Roaches the size of tortoises clung here and there, and one the size of a knightly shield hung on a landing wall. No, every apartment was a shell. Returning to ground level, I was walking against the flow again - there was a tilt to the floor. Behind the stairwell the flagstones sloped to a door so rotten it looked to have ochre feathers. Beyond this was another door which looked to have been cast from pewter. I entered with a patented Panacea parrot key.

Posh place. Windows on the ceiling. Carpet on the walls. Tiles on the floor. I'd been prepared to discover any kind of aberration but this. Corridors were hung with gold-framed paintings of baffled-looking land owners halted rigid in mud and smoke. On a dark stand was set a creepy statue of Saint Velociro in high gloss, her tilted head gleaming like liquefying wax. I poked my head into a chamber containing a skull-shaped jacuzzi, the glossy floor made of interfitted human teeth. Another room was given over to a grand mural of an eagle gliding through a canyon, which a plaque explained was symbolic of fascism moving through the democratic process. After a minute of doping out the place I cracked a small door and peered down into an illuminated basement where Heber was strapped to a table. On a large plasma screen a couple of cowboys indulged in a quickdraw which made a lot of noise and effectively destroyed the happiness of both. Murphy the Fed was leaning to look Heber in the face and spoke above the thrum of a generator. 'You're hazardous materials, kid. Concentrate because you are sick. Concentrate because you will soon die. Remember. Remember hard.'

I should have gone straight in but I wanted to leave a message first. I found a study lined with shelves that bore legal texts bound in cream imitation skin. On a wooden mount was the tusk of a senator. Pivot's desk felt like a wedding shrine of malignancy. It was the work of a few moments to prime and place the voodoo bomb in back of a small side-drawer.

Something flashed in the doorway - Murphy raised a gun and her eyebrows, as if raising a toast. It was another of those small-boned pistols she seemed to favour, I don't know which brand. She seemed amused. 'How'd you get in here, hotshot?'

'The front door.'

'It's a good enough story, I can't prove it wrong.'

There was some noise behind her - Pivot entering the apartment.

'Hey, Pale!'

Pivot appeared, taking his coat off. 'Eh, what's all this?'

'You won't believe it, I just found him playing the sleuth in here.'

'Oh? Well, he played it wrong.'

'When I get up in the morning I know I've already made at least one mistake,' I told him, edging away from the desk.

'Tie him in a chair,' Pivot said.

Murphy lowered her glint pistol a little and shot me in the right leg.

So I was distracted as she pushed me into a chair that looked to have been fashioned out of blackstrap molasses and tied my hands behind it with some sort of plastic wire. Only then did she frisk me and obtain the machine pistol and mundane mags.

Pivot stood near the desk, observing silently.

'You're in a bad mood, Pivot,' Murphy observed. 'Shall I come back when you've had time to sneer?'

'Yes,' he said, the simplicity of his reply taking the wind out of her. She left us. He scrutinised me a while. 'I see one whose face is the exhausted finale of evolution along several quite different lines: the fish, the reptile, and the snail or gastropod. Features of all these are evident in your expression. And you're a stretched wreck. What happened to your head?'

'When your plant called you and everyone else cottoned on, it was a regular jawcar jamboree.'

'Well, you've caused me considerable trouble. The round in your thigh from the purse gun, it's pocket ammo, what do the hard men call it ...?'

'A placeholder.'

'Placeholder ammo, that's it. But we could do something more permanent. My coke girl keeps her finger off the trigger only by effort of will. Her philosophy is "Don't think of it as losing a life, but as gaining a bullet." Or you could be strangled until you have the blue face of a Vedic deity. I could afford either.'

He was stood there with his hands in his pockets, wondering what to do with me. He combined stillness with precision in a way that creeped me out by suggesting he was forever held in readiness for something.

Fear - I'd forgotten what it was like, that it wasn't a decision. I tested whether I could discreetly shift the chair back by degrees. Maybe the desk itself would direct the blast the other way. I was sat hostage to Pivot and his suction-mounted morality. 'Siddown, Pivot, you're straining my neck.'

'I won't, for the moment. My ass was removed in childhood. On the plus side, the acuity of my remaining senses has increased a hundredfold. I read the gap better than almost anyone. Pattern recognition.'

'I wondered how you'd got where you are.'

'Yes, I don't really have anything else when it comes down to it. Ract has an art-collection marriage and two full-blown sons. Darkwards has his ballroom dancing or whatever he calls it. They go along that way and ignore the little jump to either side that would take them into a joke. While I have a silence barely worth coming home to, and not a ray of suspicion to enliven me.'

'All this dead stock,' I said, shucking my head at the surlyguy busts and books ignored by the yard. These vacuum-sealed keepsakes were markers of a sense of entitlement, though I'd never seen the effect in so pronounced a form. Pivot was beside himself with it. 'Nice home for the ornaments. Where do you live?'

'Exactly. No-one suspects a living creature could dwell in such a museum. So I'm at peace outside the narrowly seething bandwidth of bomb-zombies and perseverants. I wouldn't usually discuss it with someone who behaves as you have. There are two types of people in the world, Atom.'

'Two? Used to be there was over a thousand; then twelve; pretty soon they'll have it down to one. For damn sure this is America.'

'Oh, you're breaking my heart,' he said, going around the desk and sitting down. 'Are you alright? You look almost scared. Not what I expected. Your intel jacket implies you've been translated through several dimensions side-on to ours and are probably a much more exotic creature than we can see, the Atom we all know being its prick, merely.'

'I've been described as a prick, that's true.'

'Well I don't hold with urban legends about

interbeings and so forth. At this stage people will claim anything.'

'I've said nothing about it either way.'

He casually shunted a drawer on the opposite side from the primed one and retrieved a Bernardelli P-018 pistol which he held pointed negligently in my general direction, his hand resting on the desk. He looked odd with a sender, like he didn't know which end went in his gob. 'This is not really a necessary preface to what I have to do, but you'll hear me out, I know it.'

I was nauseous from the new wound and the stress of waiting for the two face salute. I'd been hoping it would be over quickly but the bastard was eloquent.

'I was unconnected, pigmentless and poor in Beerlight, which is a textbook debtropolis if you take out the headcrime. Here's a rule for remembering numbers: if it's high, it's a bill and beyond you, if it's low, it's a wage and perhaps within your grasp. The devil; the police - I could not take one and leave the other. I could have gone the British route of guns and whisky - but why not go direct? Why not trade in money? It's prestige without content but that only means you can fill in the details according to your taste.'

'Did you do anything interesting with it?'

'Ofcourse not - look around you - nobody does when it actually comes to it. By the time I realised with horror that life was no mere passing fancy, I'd grown attached to its compensatory malices. It's easiest to boost from above, and it gave me a very special feeling when I made my first bet - on a company called Ramatagen which sold novelty gun grips and textured gripcovers cloned from the owner's skin, or the owner's lover's or enemy's skin. And other stuff like hammerless placebo guns and T-shirts bearing random phrases in a language few could read. One of them said "Mind the gap", I remember.' He chuckled.

'We all find our consolation somewhere.'

'Then I needed a legitimate front, but not so legitimate that I'd seem unbelievable. At first the law and its frankly incalculable demands upon the people seemed merely another arena for career ambition. I moved among senators, semi-local officials, military generals and others in on the deception, attempting to emulate their moral words and immoral acts, and finally achieved this balance by trial and error. Out winning claws and minds, demanding money, naming for it destinations which were not always false but which never justified its source. Civilisation had purported to regard crime as a disease rather than a part of its metabolism. It was never outwardly acknowledged that certain acts might be a reasoned response. For centuries authority had thought to collapse the calculus of crime by pressing the centre of its gravity, until it realised this was also its own centre of gravity. This is only one challenge of fighting something that travels like a sand-dune, shedding cells constantly. Optimists viewed the law as no more than a desperate measure of continuity, until it began changing every week. Most then assumed the law was capricious because it varied with time, geography, funds, influence, interpretation and so on from one day to the next. But the *motives* for law are common and unchanging - that's the continuity. Take, sympathise, control. But the middle one has become a luxury. It gives nothing back.'

The play of light and shadow over his ignorance wasn't very entertaining, but so far it seemed he believed what he was saying.

'A society stemming from these principles will demand more from its people than they can give.'

'Nonsense. Each crucible of cowardice is taxed according to its compliance. And it's a good ferment for discipline. Vulgarity ties the doubtful to the state's crimes - that and the social contract, a deal made on unequal terms. Stagnation as policy - a surrogate freedom, carefully posed. Admittedly it was a society that operated well but was so finely balanced it left no room for error.'

I interrupted before anything more could emerge from the pale valve he had for a mouth. 'You're stalling for time,' I said. 'Why?'

'There's a schedule,' he said, with an almost coy smile. After a moment's reflection, he continued. I think he'd forgotten the gun. 'As a protection at street level the law is a rumour, a phantom - ghostly until invoked, and invoked only after the harm has been done. Well, you know all this. It cuts off the tail, not realising where the heart and brain are located.'

'In the cautious man, they're in the tail.'

'That's not quite what I meant. In any case, to write a law is much easier to do than explain what you mean by it. That's part of what it's for. I experimented with explaining and found I need give a reason convincing only to the simple-minded. Selling jargon as fact. Well, pretty soon lawyers outnumbered people by two to one. By this time a hundred-weight of hokum was being transferred into statute every day. Humanity, the eternally narrowing mind. I'm proud to have been present at that supreme moment when everything was illegal at last. Law was perfected - on paper, anyway. It was strange, that day. An eclipse clicked into place like an optician's test lens.'

'I remember that eclipse.'

I had been walking through a field with an antique Walther P38 in my right hand. It stung as if stuck to my hand by the blowback. Then the gun and everything else chilled. That German pistol unglued from my palm as though what I had just done was no longer my responsibility. I felt insulted, resentful. Looking back and to the left, I watched the whispering field darken as the sun closed out. I was seventeen.

'Was that the day, then?'

'I don't believe nature was aware of what had been done, but it was a hard coincidence.'

'Got bone-cold for a while.'

'The Project of the Law was completed the only way it could be. The only way the clear-eyed had ever foreseen.'

Through a yard of pain I focused on Pivot. It was like making eye-contact with a hen.

'Maybe we should empty our minds and meditate on a simple image such as a geranium.'

His silver eyebrows rose as slowly and steadily as the mercury in a thermometer. 'You are deceiving no-one, Atom.'

'Damn right.'

'Tell me then - do you believe in the hour of

inferno? The end of civilization?'

'I can't imagine why anyone would believe otherwise.'

'Dull though you are, I don't believe you can't imagine that.'

'How about you?'

'I believe it alright. Ract, Darkwards and myself have an intricate and friendly rivalry of long standing. We all three had invested in a few wildcat nerve gas stocks, and it struck us all at once that menacing a foreign country is ideal, whether it's baffled, ready or both. To wax profit from catastrophe. Once you've made a beginning, the rest generally follows on its own. We'd wager on outcomes, too. But that gets boring, and we could see where things were going. Ract and Darkwards don't have my intuition - they use a little gizmo, a fissure shunt that probes the etheric gap and extrapolates its progress. Fissure science - which isn't really prediction. Most things are obvious, really. So-called "prophecy" is easy. Optimism is the chief thing that prevents it. People can barely see the present because of that, let alone the future. And I know the medievalists determined the end of everything at 19,683 but nobody believes we'll last that long. The only variable is the method.'

Pivot was hauling several unseen planes of motivation with him like aerials, but he was unaware of them. They were notes he'd pinned to his own back. He had succumbed to the complexities of his own evasions, writhing inward like a spiral. It would be a challenge to bullseye the golden section of artifice.

'What else to do? The murder of civilization is not

even a very interesting spectacle. We see the future as a box of accidents - a terrible thing - intrusions ready to be let loose. Darkwards foresees a comet - or asteroid, I forget which. Ract finally settled on the CERN loop, cliche though it is. I can't believe in Darkwards's impending visitor. Honestly, a comet? Why accuse minerals of fate? I confidently predicted some pretty large floods. Eels and economics make strange bedfellows and my other speculations soon seemed fatuous.'

I was sure he didn't feel the reality of the enterprise, a state allowed by his belief that most facts were mere guests. 'Volcanoes aren't done for practice, you nimrod. You'd put fruit on a chain, wouldn't you?'

Pivot frowned. 'Let me pay you the courtesy of being blunt - we live in the World to End All Worlds. Earth connects little pains, and the last few connections are being made. Let's think big. The kid - Partenheimer. I heard about him before the others. I thought "Let me not repeat the sins of my forefathers, but innovate." So I bet on the kid. I couldn't leave this match of Jericho lying around. But a thing like that, there was a fierce temptation to interfere with the unfortunate creature to influence the outcome. I include myself in this. Have you guessed the odds? What, honestly, are the chances of Partenheimer ever stumbling upon an original idea, even in this city? I realised that rather quickly. So how big do I win if I force it?'

'Why win a bet that'll kill you?'

Pivot seemed despondent at having but one mouth with which to sigh. 'Why *lose* one that'll kill you? There's a theory I don't believe, that gamblers want the worst to happen, a covert suicide. But every habit started with nature. Addiction is basically anything you can't stop doing.'

'Breathing?'

'And any addiction can be ended. Life itself is a tolerated defeat. Our greatest enemy in ourselves is the wish to be alive, though in others it has worked in our favour as a handle with which to manipulate. The point is this planet's circling the drain, so ofcourse we opened a book on it. We met amid the shuffling of taxation, war and other forms of speculation but those dabblings in the unseen are completely over now, since the economy went the way of all flesh. I've got money orbiting the globe in five marked satellite accounts and it's all worthless, dead. There are no commercial vices anymore, not really. But operationally, the habit remains. You think things can ever be twisted into a neat little bundle and disposed of? Things are messy.'

'Someone else told me that recently.'

'You know that story about Charles Jamison in Atlanta, who disposed of all those invading his home?'

'Everyone knows that story.'

'Well, remember toward the end, the people going in knew they were never coming out. You've seen an animal die, Atom. You can see from its eyes, near the end, that it knows it's dying. There's an acceptance, finally. Well, here we are. At the acceptance. A prosperous doom is all we demand of the immediate future. That apocaleptic young man I have in my wine cellar - that's the doom I favour. A win is just the icing on the coffin. There.

Now you know everything about me.'

'I don't buy it. I've looked at the kid. His etheric's like Hawking radiation, carrying no information.'

'I'll take that gamble. Do you know the blast radius on him?'

'But hardly the end of everything.'

'Really. No chain reaction then, all those heads? You're a scientist now? When you connected with the kid we resolved to keep you under observation, a task which alarmed and exhausted us more than we could have expected.'

'That hitman of yours,' I said, meaning the galoot, 'he wasn't any good. He's dead now.'

'I know it,' he said sadly, and that's all.

'I predicted the collapse ten years ago. It's on record. I don't see why my involvement now would make any difference.'

'Yes, there would seem no reason not to kill you at once, what do you think?'

'I agree.'

'But I'm not going to do that,' he said with a quiet, careful quality. 'No, I'm going to lock you in with the mooncow and see how you get along. I might even leave you there and wait on the other side of town.' He handed it over like there was a bomb at the centre of the answer.

'What do you expect me to do?'

'Whatever comes to mind. Something original, even.'

The setup was iterating an infinite array of new edges as I looked at it.

'Until something happens,' he went on with a bland expression. 'The world can be decided in the middle of a moment where an insect stops. Just like that - generation dismissed.'

I was disgusted. 'What good are you, really?'

'Oh, come on. Can you really mourn the passing of this country, its pea-sized minds and planet-sized children? One half of the truth is that humanity is inescapably and demonically evil. The other half doesn't bear thinking about.'

Pivot's face was blank. But he was grinning just beyond the edge of what I could see. I braced too late for the blast, a cobalt flare leaving a fuzzy blot in mid-air, haloed pink with blood particulates. I had something painful in my eye. The shelves were burning. I was laying back on my tied hands and pieces of chair. Everything was jumbled up. The scorch was quickly overcome with the sick sweetness of black blood and offal.

Murphy the Fed leaned in very close, her yellow corona of hair zinging my skin as she cooed, 'Oh, baby, you lost an eye.'

She was trying to stand me up, cutting the bindings. Poisonous pain flashed up and down the left side of my done-for body. At the moment of eruption Pivot had reflexively squeezed the trigger, smacking a traditional round into my left shoulder. I had almost zero articulation in the left arm and a swollen half-hand on the end of it. Presumably I had taken a bit of desk in my left eye. With the right I saw some of Pivot behind the charred desk. He was burst like a popped corn. A portion of him was dashed up the wall. His ribs were blown open in a way that made him resemble a stamped centipede.

Murphy was wagging her chibi gun at the door. 'Why?' I asked.

'Because I'm worth it.'

I was walking busted and hunched. 'You called Pivot in.'

'So? And everyone else followed, but we got him.'

'Everyone else is Betty.'

'Eh? Why?'

'The DD goggles, as standard. The rally attack was one group, apart from Pivot's Mexican. The cops couldn't draw the factions together - Betty's my bet.'

She thought about that. 'Alright. Probably right. So what.'

I was done. She brought the kid up and led us out the sculpted door and the rotten one and then into the morning rain. My last Jade shot was fading and I was throttling either down or up - probably up. The day was working me over with white skies.

Out of the vanishing point a skimming chevron was shadowing the road. I thought it was something stuck on my remaining eye, but it grew to become Strobe the security swan. Murphy saw it a second after me and fired two shots with the purse pistol. I was about to push the kid behind the Mantarosa, invisible to the Fed. But before I could flinch in that direction, the swan swooped over, dropping a gold holographic bomb through the car's torn roof. The windows clouded and the car disappeared. This wasn't a fractal evaporation - it had switched off like a light. I realised it was a cloaking effect, but denial had never worked in me.

'Oh wow,' said the Fed, standing beside me. It was obvious she could see the car clearly.

What was the true thing I would not want to

believe? I approached the area hesitantly as if blindfolded, until my hand touched hot metal. The new perception poured down with the rain, filtering gradually into place. The car lay visible in front of me, warped open like a seashell. Its innards were ash.

My way home was obliterated. It would be easier to unlock a door closed in a photograph.

'What will I do now, Gamete? What do I do?'

The Fed was unimpressed. 'So you lost your car, so what?'

'It wasn't a car. It was a door.'

'A door.'

'I'm stuck with you people. I can't believe it.'

'Calm down.'

So I was fated to die on stage among actors who couldn't shake off their roles.

4

THE BATTLE OF BETTY'S FORT

Standing in molten rain, my heart springing leaks. My skin felt like ground glass. I wanted out, to be redeemed from the abyss of disguise.

Murphy loaded the kid in the front passenger seat of her car and me in the back, where I started to push off a thick layer of myself that I had worn like an invisible rubber suit. With every push the car's engine threatened to stall out. The private detective analog had always been strange in a town where a living body was more incongruous than a dead one. Now the whole accretion was sloughing off in one go. The Fed frowned back at me.

'Don't worry,' I said, 'it's worse than it looks.' There was another clamp of pain and the ambience guttered. The longest night of the mind. 'It doesn't count if it's easy.'

Razors of light across the brain. It was visceral bloody detox.

By the time we pulled up at Betty's Fort everything felt brighter, but it still hurt. It wasn't meant to be a cure. Parked outside Betty's was a stretch limo apparently made entirely of bone. I was thirsty. I went into the Fort like a whipped hunchback.

A profitless pat-down in the carbine corridor - the gunsels seemed nervous, glancing at the chamber entrance beyond which voices were nattering: 'The end won't occur because an innocent mind desires it. If there's no-one home and no lights on, we *turn* them on.'

The Fed led me and the kid into Betty's throne room. The gunsels stayed behind, big steel doors meeting to complete the raised design of a trilobite. This creature revolved once, clanking as the door locked.

It was a little confab of the city fathers. Betty, Blince, Ract, Darkwards.

Betty leaned forward from her beetle-black throne. 'So you're defecting, Murphy. Where's Pivot?'

'Undertakers' arrest.'

'Dead? Time to act thunderstruck, everyone.'

'And this one had some sort of phantom miscarriage in the car.'

Betty squinted. 'Atom, is it?'

'I'm nobody,' I said. 'You'll be dealing with me now.'

'No name so death can't find you I suppose? We'll call you Atom, dear.'

The giant and the dwarf were sat on the kevlar couch. Ract was paging around in a lifestyle magazine for the upper classes called *Immune*, but he glanced up when I was mentioned. 'This one-eared bravo - he's really the shamus? Looks a bit queasy.'

Blince was at the drinks cabinet behind them. He seemed completely at ease, even half amused. 'He used to be one tough customer,' he remarked, building an October Surprise with his left hand. He had some kind of bandage arrangement at his shoulder and his right arm in a sling. 'Seems kinda ragged and emotional today.'

'You're rather more manlike than the galoot described you,' said the giant in a mild tone, tilting his big log-like face at me.

'He was socked in the eye by a bit of Pivot, I think,' said the Fed, with a smirk.

'Nasty bump on the old noggin, eh?' said the giant in a louder tone, as if to a child. His apparently upholstered forehead shone in the artificial light. 'My name's Darkwards. Like it?'

'Not much.'

'Yes, well yours isn't up to much either.'

'Get rid of it.'

'Enough of this nonsense,' Betty said pleasantly, and stroked her pet ganglion.

Without looking up from his magazine the dwarf muttered 'Pivot and his intrepid cheats have nearly damned us all, as usual.'

'Oh, come,' said the giant mildly. 'We recognised him as one whose ethical dexterity allowed him almost anything at any time. Why condemn that quality now?'

'Generally speaking I regarded him as an equal, so long as his face was obscured and he didn't interfere. But he never hid his indifference to my attempts to manipulate him. Just sat there eating a fruit and staring at me as I went on. Incredibly annoying.'

Darkwards gave a sick and quiet chuckle.

'What about the Mexican?' Blince asked.

'Who cares?' Betty declared. 'A man who sees intelligence as ugly paunch and denies that his body is anything more than a combat chassis. His mind embodies a human mind in miniature. Good luck to him.'

Blince agreed without enthusiasm.

The kid was wandering, looking at the curios and bookshelves.

'We're in lockdown,' announced Betty. 'And if a new personality signature does show its face, these sentinels will activate.' She looked to the Mission-style gun emplacements on either side of her throne. 'It's good, gentlemen, that we all joined forces at last - formally. So much noise and waste at the Gate. Our core values entwine. See the structure of material power, Mr Atom? It's guns all the way up.'

'The blonde kid,' said Blince. 'He's Partenheimer?'

'Yes, the Head Perilous. Come here, Heber.'

The kid put aside a Gamete book and walked over to the front of Betty's throne-stage, looking up at her.

'See all this?' Betty said to him. 'These days entitlement can be manufactured - after all, who's keeping track? You'll stay here with me a little while.'

The expected gratitude was unforthcoming. Heber looked up at her like a hollow saint. The mercy of Betty's leopardskin philosophy seemed to stretch a little this way and that, then relax.

'Well,' she said with a control that sounded prim. 'I'm good at a certain kind of negotiation. You understand that word? I've been doing this my whole life. Just this. The market and its monarchy of confidence. You would have found it an excellent consolation. Remunerative dissonance once enhanced the flow of life, but it became so lopsided it broke. Trade became a labour of mourning. The pattern persists without content. How simple it all is.'

Betty stopped, looking at him.

'Little Prince Myshkin is blank. I'm speaking to myself.'

'He's definitely Partenheimer,' said the Fed. Stood next to a big plant vase near the door, she looked a little wide-eyed and out of her depth.

'What do you want, a medal?'

'Or the value I'd trade it for.'

'He's a dud,' I said, 'the balloon standard in stupidity. Even more than Blince over there.'

'This phoney gumshoe's playing you!' shouted the Fed.

'Your glittering conjecture tells me nothing.'

'Who does he work for?' asked Ract, looking up to scowl. 'Eh, you? Who do you work for?'

'I don't understand the question,' I said. Ract had seemed to be damn near frothing with disinterest but he and Darkwards were basically of a piece. I detected some acoustic difference between their positions but that was all. In fact the chamber gave me the feel of an intertidal zone of motives, all together in avarice. 'Love isn't friendly. And I'm full of love.'

Betty's pet ganglion let out a scionic squeal.

'My spine wants to know how an alibi so frequently disproved is still exalted.'

'Cos he's a goddamn throwback, why it is,' said Blince. 'Headcrime, artcrime, installation capers. The currency's spent.'

Murphy the Fed piped up, frowning. 'Listen, old timer. I missed alot of that and I like to think there's still some wine in the bottle.'

Betty was stood forward with a Jericho out of nowhere and I heard a crack. A beauty spot on Murphy's forehead started spurting and she sat down sadly in a corner. I felt bad for her last words, for what she'd missed and wouldn't realise. Some unfairness is a hole, pure and simple. After firing, Betty stepped back appraisingly like an artist. She hadn't shot anyone in years. This whole setup was some sort of special occasion.

Blince had reflexively pulled an AMT pistol at the shot, and stood with it aimed left-handed and awkward at Betty Criterion.

'Chief Blince,' said Betty, sitting back in her throne. 'For whatever reason, the fates saw fit to put you and your immense interior at the disposal of the state. You could have refused.'

'I could.'

'Some people have that wisdom. Very few. Not you.'

'So what if I am? - Which I doubt!' he exclaimed confusedly. 'And what's the gun for?'

'Emphasis. I've put mine up. Do the same, please.'

Obedient as a match on the third strike, Blince put the gun up.

Blood began to lake outwards around Murphy.

'I might declare it the slaying of the season,' remarked Ract without inflection.

The kid had wandered back to the book shelves. I stood like an idiot. It was the most lateral standoff I'd ever been a part of. I wondered if they were waiting for her to give a signal.

'What's coming to you, Atom,' Blince muttered. He snipped the tip from his cigar, looked at it, put it between his lips, lit up. 'Will arrive.'

Instead of a heart he had a huge shut eye.

'Your timetables for the absolute are insulting,' I said.

'The schedule's published and the tickets have been sold,' said Betty. Her pet spine had shuffled off when the shooting started but I noticed she was still dandling the Jericho pistol from her knee. 'Humanity has so far set up a rather makeshift torment and there is still much to do. Its short memory allows it to forget even its own apocalypse, its escalating terms in hell. Re the nuclear stuff they've been smug since the big deal. The EMP wave five years ago knocked out a city and nothing was learnt. Same with the quakes. It isn't funny and it isn't clever.'

'I still contend the first of Feb's the date for that asteroid of yours,' Ract snicked aside at Darkwards. 'That infernal marvel of velocity'll have everyone holding their bones but my atomic loop'll get there first.'

'I'm talking about a comet, as you well know. A scabby red card, a timely bubo. We had it coming.'

'Let's hope and pray the world will be assailed with every kind of cataclysm and upheaval. At

177

the same time, I mean, rather than spread out as people expect. It will be exactly like a race, neck and neck!'

'My asteroid has it in the bag, Mr Ract.'

'You see?' said Betty, turning to me. 'We're just protecting our interests.'

'Nothing can do that at this stage. Are you *really* unaware of it? The bet's off.'

'What's that?' Ract snapped, dropping his magazine.

'Taking us all by storm are you,' said Betty. Her eyes were nonsignifying insets. 'Smashing upwards into our lives.'

'Maybe I am.'

'What's this about the bet? What happened, *who* won it?'

'None of you.'

'Whaddya mean?'

'It's simple. You made a bet as to the method by which civilisation will end. But everything you've done, everything you've said, thought, observed, should have made it clear to you that civilisation has already ended.'

Ice cold behind the face, Ract glared at me. 'Shamus, this explanation you seem to have coughed out of your ass has done nothing to reassure me.'

After a dead silence, Blince piped up. 'Huh. He had me going for a minute.'

'He's quite right,' said Betty. 'It's over. And let's not point the forearm of blame. Pivot didn't realise either. Goes to show you can't subpoena wisdom. I used to think it would fall amid a battle, with governments clutching at what they might lose to the people. As it turned out, everyone just kept pretending, as best they could amid the ashes. Here in Beerlight it's the comforting old gangland modality. Parts of the Fadlands have gone full pasta, as you probably know. Humanity has tanked. Get used to it. It might be called its "death" or "destruction" were these not somewhat grandiose names for so small an affair: an empire falling silently as snow on old bones. Just another self-vanquished species.'

'But the bet!' Ract shouted.

'Forget what you think you know about the apocalypse. It'll destroy the head, the torso, and other cherished misconceptions about the human body. Something else is clearly at stake. Raise your sights, gentlemen. The world. The bet is the world.'

Ract and Darkwards turned to look at each other, then back at Blince, who nodded.

'Agreed.'

'That's why we're here, after all.' She smiled slowly, almost realistically.

'I don't believe this,' I said.

'What?' Betty asked. 'It's such a slight matter. The end of the world. It's come rather late, I'm afraid. But more interesting than some breakaway empire.'

She had a gun and was taking her sweet time about shooting me. They were holding back, waiting on something. Which had happened before.

'Get to the point.'

'Say what you mean, Atom.'

'I mean, quit stalling. I think that'd be the local term. What are you counting on? What's the deal here?'

There was a sudden bang as the kid dropped a bound book on the floor - he bent to pick it up. When I looked back at the others I saw they were coming back from a bad scare, covering up.

They were at once hopeful and terrified of the innocent opulence that might propagate all at once behind his eyes. I could not honestly bring these thoughts to any other conclusion. The notion burned phosphorescent inside. My heart was burning with grief and anger. 'This sort of thing never ends well,' I said. There was silence. 'Aren't you going to ask what I mean?'

'Not a chance,' said Ract, looking scared - his eyes flicked to the kid.

'Oh, you people have had value out of me,' I told them. 'I've done everything wrong this time. Following leads. *Following!* What a chump! Now you fuck up my window out of here. I don't know how I'm getting home. And worst of all, you're *boring* me!'

Betty was staring straight at the kid, her claws clenched to the arms of her throne.

'I'm sick of all this. My deepest contradictions are of one accord when compared to you alien fucking smithereens.' I barely knew what I was saying. I was seething. My body shook. *'MUST I REALLY TAKE CARE OF THIS MYSELF?'*

The connective tissue between the walls and floor seemed to contract.

'You're standing there like a gunslinger,' Darkwards said with a sort of sniggering gasp. 'You'll have to reach deep to make a difference here.'

I swept the Hand of Glory from the etheric

holster and aimed it into the midst of them. The ground hardened under my feet. I understood even as I squeezed the trigger that they had all changed their bets. Everything on the kid.

The whirr of acceleration as the unfamiliar gun powered up for ignition scared me and then it was extruding baffles and riveted armatures and reversing pulsations up my arm. The cylinder rotated through a dozen modes I didn't recognise. Threads of blue light were running along its fluted cowling as it Swiss-Armied open, enclosing my arm like armour and flipping out six circular projections like directional propellor guards. The weight belied the fact that I was now holding something bigger than a Harley-Davidson.

As if its understanding of the scene led to a terrifyingly compressed urgency, it exploded upon the roomful of gaping targets. I think I saw Darkwards jerk with a bolting charge of realisation and then there were leaping outlines in blinding incandescence. Being in back of that gun was like being on a rollercoaster. Shrill blasts of backdraft batted from the six muzzles as they exchanged sinewless patterns of swooping matter, motive particles shooting in vertices, gathering denser compression until it all locked together in a thunderclap of mutuality.

I dropped the gun.

Betty, Blince, Ract and Darkwards seemed to be gone.

A massive, gutty beachball stood in the centre of the throne room. In its fleshy surface, four faces stretched like melted cheese. Poking from one was a cigar, still smoking.

'Let's go back over this thing a little,' said Blince.

The pyramidal gun drones on either side of Betty's throne came to life, firing upon the group anomaly. It exploded in a storm of blood and shredded matter.

It was messy. Me and the kid were red statues in a red room.

'Well,' I said, dazed. 'You alright?'

I went over and slapped him on his slimy shoulder.

'I'm not much used to this sort of thing.' I looked at the red room, my red arms. 'Thank god I was disgusted with those bastards, or I might have been part of that. Ah, I'm all *verklempt.*'

The kid seemed overcome by it all. His eyes had a surprised look of imminence like he was about to sneeze. I didn't immediately realise it was the confluence of nitrophages in his uterine mind. Then he looked at me.

'Oh.'

The air around Heber was starting to wrinkle, bunching inward. Then it tore in places, light blazing through like pain. Gravity became precarious.

'Oh, kid,' I said. 'I'm sorry.'

He smiled faintly. The world bent open, ripping.

I was incredulous with light.

Lightning Source UK Ltd.
Milton Keynes UK
175100UK00001B/8/P

9 780956 567727